camp CONFIDENTIAL

Natalie's Secret

by Melissa J. Morgan

SCHOLASTIC INC.

New York Toronto London Auckland Sydney
Mexico City New Delhi Hong Kong Buenos Aires

ISBN 0-439-75673-1

12 11 10 9 8 7 6 5 4 3 2 1   5 6 7 8 9 10/0

Printed in the U.S.A.   40

First Scholastic printing, April 2005

camp CONFIDENTIAL

Natalie's Secret

chapter
ONE

Dear Hannah,

Hey there! I can't remember the last time I picked up a pen and paper to write an honest-to-goodness letter, but desperate times call for desperate measures, I guess. I have no idea whether or not there will be any computer access at—ugh, it's too torturous to even think about—CAMP. Mom insists that it won't be as backwoods as I'm expecting, but at this point I'm not sure I trust her! I mean, really—sending me away to Nowheresville, Pennsylvania, for eight weeks? She is obviously having some sort of mental breakdown, and I'm the one who's going to suffer!

You're so lucky your parents are taking you to Europe. I know you're not that excited about all of the touring around (dusty old paintings and all) but seriously, it has to be better than painting clay pots and identifying different poisonous leaves and whatever else they do at camp all summer long. Promise me you'll take lots of pics of your gorgeous self being all cool and sophisticated in front of the Mona Lisa, Big Ben, the Trevi fountain . . .

Have I mentioned that I'm way jealous?

I think we're about an hour from Camp Lake-puke—joy—so I'm going to put down my pen and start "rethinking my attitude," as Mom suggested. She is totally

convinced that the fresh air will do me good.
I pointed out that if fresh air was so
important, we wouldn't live in Manhattan,
but somehow she didn't see things my way.

There is a girl sitting two seats in front
of me with awesome clips in her hair. Like
little sequins or something. She has the
thickest mess of curly red hair I've ever seen.
And I bet it's her natural color. Anyway,
the barrettes are promising. Maybe I'll go
make friends. Or not.

You better miss me! Cross your fingers
that this summer is as painless as possible and
that we're back in NYC before we even
know it (even if it means school again)!

xoxo,
Nat

7

Natalie signed her letter, folded the crisp lavender sheet of paper into a neat square, and tucked it into the front pocket of her bag with a sigh. Her envelopes and stamps were all packed away in her trunk, which had been shipped separately a week before. Hopefully, her things would be waiting for her when she arrived at camp.

Camp Lakeview. It was all Natalie could do not to shudder at the thought of it. To say that she was not interested in nature was a severe understatement. In fact, Natalie was pretty sure that she was actually allergic to nature. Natalie and her mother lived in the "concrete jungle"—the coolest, most interesting city in the world—New York. The closest Natalie ever came to the great outdoors was when she and her friends went Rollerblading in Central Park on weekends. And that was just fine by her.

Most summers, Natalie would take special classes that were offered by local private schools. She'd study painting or drawing or writing or dancing. The rest of the time, she and her friends would hang out, shop, see movies . . . it was awesome. But not this summer. This summer, Natalie's mother had to travel to Italy. She was an art buyer, and she needed to scout out new pieces for her gallery. Natalie had begged to go with her, but Natalie's mom was firm. "Camp will be good for you," she had said. "A change of pace. A chance to meet different types of people."

"What's wrong with the people I know now?" Natalie had asked.

Her mother had laughed. "Nothing, of course. Your friends are wonderful, sweetie. But everyone you know lives in the same neighborhood as you and goes to the same school. You even go to the same tennis lessons and music programs. It will be good for you to broaden your horizons."

"I like my horizons narrow," Natalie had protested stubbornly. But her mother's word was final.

That conversation had taken place five months ago. Now, Natalie's mind raced as the stuffy charter bus she rode careened down the highway toward Camp Lakeview. Endless grassy pastures dotted the landscape, and she had even seen a few cows and sheep grazing. *Sheep*, for Pete's sake. Was this what her mother meant about broader horizons?

She could go home now, right?

Natalie glanced at the other kids on the bus. She couldn't believe that there wasn't anyone on the bus as miserable as she was, but looking around, most of the other kids were grinning away, laughing, talking to one another . . . Natalie didn't know a soul here. She wasn't especially shy, but she also wasn't thrilled at the prospect of having to make all new friends. Her own friends were cool, and other than Hannah, they were all back in New York City taking a drama intensive offered by a special high school for teenage actors. Everyone was there. Including Kyle Taylor. Kyle Taylor who had, it should be noted, promised to write Natalie over the summer. *That is, if he doesn't forget about me*, she decided. *Which, how could he not, what with me out in the wilderness with the lions and tigers and bears and whatever.*

I should have asked Dad to talk to Mom for me, Natalie thought glumly. *He would have let me go to acting school, definitely.* But as quickly as the thought had popped up,

Natalie pushed it out of her mind. Talking to her father was Out of the Question. He and her mother had split up when Natalie was only four years old, and even though Natalie knew her father loved her, they didn't talk very often. It was hard to be in touch with him because . . . no, she wasn't going to think about it. Talking to her father was, at least for right now, a non-option, and therefore, she'd just have to pray that Camp Lake-puke, as she had come to think of the place, wasn't as bad as she feared.

Natalie snapped out of her little daze to see Cool Barrette Girl smiling at her. Well, in her general direction, anyway. Natalie took her chances and smiled back. Success. Barrette Girl stood up from her seat, stretched, and wove her way back to where Natalie sat.

"Hi," she said, still grinning, "I'm Grace Matthews. I'm from New Jersey. Montvale. It's in the north, right by the George Washington Bridge." She stuck out her hand to shake, which seemed a little weird to Natalie. The only people she knew who shook hands were grown-ups—but, hey—she wasn't about to start turning away friendly faces. She reached out her own hand toward Grace.

"I'm Natalie Goode," she said.

"You're new, right?" Grace asked. "I was here last summer."

"Yeah, I'm from Manhattan, so, um, I'm not so used to summer camp," Natalie said. She realized she was babbling. What was wrong with her? She didn't usually get nervous around new people. But this, this whole camp *thing* was totally new and strange to her. "So, yeah, I'm new," she finished, feeling sort of lame.

"You'll love it," Grace assured her. "There are a few

other kids from the city here, and they, like, love it even more than the rest of us. I think 'cause they're not used to, you know, trees."

"Oh, hey, no—we've got tons of trees where I come from. I mean, there's a tree right outside my building," Natalie said, hoping Grace would get that she was kidding.

Grace burst out laughing. "Oh, well then, you're ready for the nature shack!" she agreed, shaking out her bright red hair and quickly pinning it right back up. "How old are you?"

"Eleven," Natalie said.

"Oh, cool, me too," Grace replied. "Hey—maybe we'll be in the same bunk! There are eight bunks in every division—four girls' bunks and four boys'. If you're in mine, I can introduce you to everyone. Well, I mean, I'd introduce you, anyway, but you know—it'd be cool if we were in the same bunk!"

"Yeah, cool," Natalie agreed, hoping she didn't sound as unexcited as she felt. She knew that trees and new people weren't such a bad thing, but somehow, she just couldn't get her enthusiasm together.

"Hey, Grace," shouted a voice from the front of the bus, "we're gonna play hangman!"

Grace rolled her eyes, pretending to be impatient. "Right, hangman. Really important stuff. Do you want to play?" she offered.

Natalie shook her head. "Nah, I'm going to just relax a little bit. Prepare myself for all the trees and stuff."

"Gotcha," Grace said, giggling again. "Well, if you change your mind, I'm just a few seats ahead." She made her way up toward the chattering girls, leaving Natalie alone with her own thoughts again.

Seated in the window seat next to Natalie was a very quiet girl with long, jet-black hair. This girl was hunched over a notebook, scribbling away intently. She hadn't said one word to anyone since they boarded two hours ago, just opened up her notebook and retreated into her own world. She hadn't even looked up when Grace came over to say hi. Natalie couldn't decide how she felt about her seatmate. The fact that this girl was dressed in jeans and a ripped black T-shirt while everyone else was in shorts and tank tops could either be cool or weird. The same went for her refusal to look up and make conversation. Natalie was dying to know what she was writing in her notebook. Lots of her friends from New York were into art and writing and liked to dress differently and wear cool jewelry. So this girl could definitely be sort of cool. Or she could be a total weirdo. It could really go either way.

"All right, guys, listen up!" came a loud voice from the front of the bus. A tall, lanky guy with dark, curly hair pulled into a ponytail stood and addressed them all. He looked a little stressed—a few stray curls had escaped his ponytail and were standing at attention on the top of his head—but also good-natured and friendly. "If I didn't meet you before, I'm meeting you now. I'm Pete, and I'm going to be working in the mess hall this summer!" This announcement brought forth a round of booing and hissing, but Pete waved it off. "None of that," he laughed, "or you don't know what I'll put in the 'tuna surprise.'"

Natalie cringed. "Call me old-fashioned, but I prefer my tuna without any surprises," she mumbled. She was surprised to hear a snort from her right and looked over to see her seatmate stifling a chuckle.

"Agreed," the girl said. She quickly went back to her notebook, as if afraid she had said too much. Natalie was so shocked by the sudden burst of conversation that she forgot to reply. But she didn't have time to, anyway, because Pete was still talking.

"We'll be arriving at camp in about a half hour or so," he explained. "When we get there, you'll come off the bus. There will be a counselor waiting to tell you what bunk you're in and where you're going. So the first thing you want to do is go to your bunk. If fate has been kind to us—and I've got my fingers crossed here—then your trunk or any other luggage you may have shipped will be waiting for you there. You'll meet your counselors and your bunkmates, unpack, and have your bunk meetings." He paused. "Any questions?"

"Yeah," shouted a rowdy boy from the back of the bus. "What's for dinner tonight?"

"Cookout!" Pete said. He sounded highly thrilled at the prospect.

The entire bus erupted into a chorus of cheers. Natalie stared at her fellow campers incredulously. *Cookout?* she wondered. She could not for the life of her understand why something as simple as a barbecue was eliciting such a response. *Sushi, maybe*, she thought. *Hamburgers . . . not so much.*

She glanced to her right again. Her seatmate was still engrossed in her notebook, completely unimpressed by the news of the cookout. Well, that was one thing they had in common, at least. Natalie folded her arms across her chest and leaned back, sighing again.

It was going to be a long eight weeks.

chapter TWO

Natalie rested comfortably in bed, her head cradled by soft down pillows, her body on a mattress that was just the right balance of firm and squishy. The room, a log cabin similar to one Natalie had stayed in on a recent ski trip with her mother, was air-conditioned to the perfect temperature. *Hmmm, I didn't think there would be air-conditioning at camp,* Natalie thought. *I could get used to roughing it.*

Maybe there's going to be sushi for dinner, she thought. *And then afterward we can make frozen-yogurt sundaes.*

"Natalie, wake up," her counselor said, leaning over and nudging her gently. "We're leaving for our field trip in just a few minutes. We'll be going to New York, to the Met."

The Metropolitan Museum? New York? Natalie thought. That was another pleasant surprise. She was pretty sure that Camp Lakeview was at least three hours away from New York. *Some field trip.*

"Natalie, wake up," the voice said again. The owner of the voice nudged her again, this time not so gently.

"Ow," Natalie said, rubbing her shoulder. "Come on! Quit it."

"Sorry," the voice said, "but we're here. I think you have to get off the bus now."

Here? Natalie peeled her eyes open. *Here.* As in, Camp Lakeview. They had arrived. Natalie groaned.

"Yeah, you were sleeping pretty soundly. You dropped off just after the announcement about the cookout tonight. I take it you're not big into red meat."

"Whatever," Natalie said, rubbing her eyes and feeling grouchy. She looked over to see who was talking to her. It was her seatmate, the maybe-cool notebook girl. "I guess not," she admitted, feeling bad about being so touchy. It wasn't this girl's fault she was so anti-camp.

"Yeah, well, I'm a vegetarian. I get it," the girl said. "My name's Alyssa."

"I'm Natalie," Natalie said with a little smile. A little smile was about the best she could do at the moment.

"I know, I heard you introduce yourself to that girl Grace. You said it was your first summer here. Mine too. And I'm also eleven. So maybe we're in the same bunk."

"There are four bunks of eleven-year-olds," Natalie pointed out. A look of disappointment flickered across Alyssa's face, and Natalie worried that she had unintentionally hurt the girl's feelings. *Nice people skills, Nat,* she scolded herself. "But, you know, I hope we are!" she said quickly. She was relieved to see a smile return to Alyssa's face.

Natalie and Alyssa gathered their things and stepped off the bus. It took a moment for Natalie's eyes to adjust to the bright sunlight, and when they did, she gasped in surprise. Whatever her expectations had been of camp, she wasn't prepared for *this.*

In a word, it was chaos. All the buses were lined up, parked, in an open field. Just beyond all the buses, though, was a clearing lined with balloons and enormous, hand-lettered signs with greetings like "Welcome, Lakeview Campers!" and "Happy Summer!" And girls and boys anywhere from age eight to sixteen were wandering back and forth, some looking eager, some looking as confused as she felt. In the midst of the crowd were older people—counselors and staff, Natalie assumed—waving clipboards and shouting instructions into megaphones. It was all extremely perky, Natalie thought. She wasn't sure how she felt about that. Come to think of it, she was practically still half-asleep.

"WHAT'S YOUR NAME?" A clipboard was thrust under Natalie's nose. She followed the clipboard up and found herself looking into the face of an older woman wearing a fluorescent orange sun visor and a stripe of zinc down her nose. *No one* in New York City wore sun visors. At least, not anyone Natalie knew.

"Natalie. Natalie Goode," she managed, after taking a moment to recover.

The woman looked at her clipboard briskly. "Natalie Goode. New York City."

"That's me."

"Well, Natalie, I'm Helen Proctor. I'm the camp nurse. Right now, I'm helping all the campers find their bunks. You, my friend, are in the third division. Kathleen is your division head. You'll love her. And you're in bunk 3C," the woman told her. "Your counselor is Julie and Marissa will be your CIT."

"CIT?" Natalie asked. Was that anything like the CIA? Or NPR? Probably not.

"Counselor-in-training," Helen explained. "It's the division between the oldest campers and the counselors. The CITs wait tables in the mess hall, and they're each assigned to one bunk."

Natalie nodded. "Cool," she said. At least, it sounded cool. Time would tell.

Helen leaned forward, crouching next to Natalie. She pointed toward a thin dirt path leading away from the field. "If you follow that path, you'll see that it curves around. That path runs through the main part of the camp—the bunks, the mess hall, and the rec hall. Head down that path and stick to the left. The fourth bunk you pass will be 3C." She patted Natalie on the shoulder reassuringly.

"Great," Natalie said, unconvinced. "Um, thanks." She looked around to see where Alyssa had gone, but she had already disappeared. There could be no more putting it off. She was here at Camp Lakeview, on her way to the bunk.

While on the bus, Natalie had somehow managed to convince herself that camp might not actually be that bad. She had even dreamed of bunks like log cabins, cute little cottages like the ones she and her mother stayed in when they went on vacation. But now, suddenly, her mouth was dry and she felt sweaty and nervous. She willed herself to relax. *Your bunkmates will be cool,* she told herself. *There's going to be a girl there who's into just the same kind of music that you like, and there will be someone who's way funny and wears the same size clothes as you, and you can share jeans and give each other manicures. And you can take a nice, long shower after you've unpacked so you can start to feel human again.* She imagined herself digging her thick terrycloth robe out from her trunk and hanging it just outside a nice shower stall. She'd turn the water on full blast and melt away the travel grime. Then she'd change into her most comfortable track pants and snuggle under her covers until dinnertime. Maybe she'd even blow her hair out—*first day of camp, and all.*

The path curved around, and Natalie hung a left, just like Helen had told her to. Almost immediately, she came upon a cluster of . . .

No. No way.

It just wasn't possible. There was no *way* that these crumbling, paint-chipped shacks were the *bunks*. As in, where she was expected to *live* for eight whole weeks!

The ramshackle structures couldn't have been less similar to the log cabins of Natalie's fantasies. They barely looked like they would make it through the summer, they were so dilapidated. The bunks were constructed of flimsy-looking planks of wood that had probably been a uniform color once upon a time, but age and weather had rendered them a dull and faded shade of gray. "Windows" were screens without shutters or panes. Natalie wondered what happened when it rained.

Swallowing hard, she counted to the fourth building and stepped up toward it slowly. *Looks can be deceiving,* she reminded herself. *Don't judge a book by its cover.* She racked her brain for any other clichés that could offer any small bit of comfort. Someone had tacked a big pink posterboard to the front door. "WELCOME, BUNK 3C," it said. The sign was decorated with glitter and lots of girls' names. It was hard for Natalie to imagine that in just a few moments all those names would be actual people— people she'd be sharing one big room with for two whole months. She had never shared a room before, ever, other than for a sleepover party. *Just do it*, she decided. It was time to just jump in. *Here goes nothing*, she thought, and pushed the door open, stepping into bunk 3C.

Natalie couldn't believe that her own mother had paid money for her to stay here. Or that there were girls who were looking *forward* to living in a bunk. She didn't know how she was going to make it.

The door clacked shut behind her, bouncing on its hinges. The fact that the door didn't have a knob or any other lock-type mechanism did not escape her. But she couldn't dwell on such matters. Because the bunk itself had many, many other problems.

Six bunk beds were lined up on either side of the small, square room. Two single beds were arranged just beyond the main bunk "area," obviously intended for the counselors. The thin, stained mattresses bore little resemblance to the fabulous bed she'd been dreaming of. And sleeping on a top bunk was clearly out of the question. She'd never fallen out of bed, but she sure wasn't eager to tempt fate from eight feet in the air. The top bunks had some sort of railing, but she wasn't interested in taking chances.

The floor was wooden, scuffed, and looked likely to splinter off. She thought gratefully of having packed her striped, rubber flip-flops. Crooked wooden cubbies were built into the walls, obviously intended for the campers' belongings. She was supposed to unpack her clothes and just leave them in open shelves for everyone to see? Wouldn't they get dusty or dirty or . . . well, she couldn't really think of anything too terrible that would happen to her stuff, but still—it seemed like a bad idea.

Thinking again of her grand plan to shower, Natalie cautiously made her way into the bathroom. *How bad could it be?* she asked herself. She was instantly sorry that she had.

Oh. That bad.

It wasn't the sticky, stained floor that bothered her (she did have those striped flip-flops, after all). Neither was it the no-frills row of stall showers facing the far back wall. Oh, sure, she could see even from the doorway how mildewed and moldy those curtains were. The fact that the toilet-paper rolls were soggy with humidity wasn't a great concern.

No, what freaked Natalie out was the toilet. Specifically, the state of one toilet—one of only *two* that twelve girls were expected to share. On top of this toilet was the hugest, slimiest, squirmiest, and all-out grossest spider Natalie had ever seen. Even if someone had been able to kill this spider—and frankly, she wasn't really sure that that would even be possible—its spidery, icky essence would live on. On the toilet seat.

Well, she just wouldn't use the bathroom. Ever.

Natalie crossed to one of the sinks that stood in a row on the opposite wall of the shower stalls. She glanced at her face in the mirror—no good news there—and splashed some water across her cheeks. She patted her face and walked back into the sleeping area of the bunk.

"So, you're Natalie? Or are you Alyssa or Chelsea or Grace?"

Natalie looked over to see a petite blond girl talking to her. "I'm Julie," the girl continued, smiling widely. "I'm going to be your counselor this summer."

Julie had bright, clear blue eyes and freckles covering every visible square inch of skin. Her hair was short, straight, and shiny. Her skin was scrubbed clean, and her complexion was fresh. Julie looked like a very "perky" person. Natalie had her doubts about "perky" people and couldn't help but be slightly wary of Julie. But of course, she had to at least try, didn't she?

"I'm Natalie," Natalie said, introducing herself. She coaxed what she hoped was a passable smile to her face.

"Right, I knew I had a one-in-four shot because the tri-state buses just arrived. So it was either you or Alyssa or Grace or Chelsea. Chelsea's from Pennsylvania," Julie explained.

Natalie was a little relieved that Julie was just organized, not a mind reader. "A girl named Alyssa was on my bus. So was a Grace. They're both eleven. So it's probably them," she reasoned, feeling a little more relaxed to know that there would be at least two people in her bunk who weren't *total* strangers.

"Well, in that case, I'm sure they'll be here soon," Julie said. "I arranged everyone's luggage—I mean, the stuff that was shipped beforehand, anyway—in front of a bed. Yours is right there," Julie said, indicating the second bunk in the right. "Alex will be in the same bunk bed, so since you're here first, I guess you get to choose top or bottom. Lucky you."

"Well, I personally prefer the bottom. But what if Alex does, too?" Natalie worried.

Julie laughed. "These things usually work themselves out. If Alex is dead-set on a bottom bunk, there will definitely be someone willing to trade with her. You'd be surprised how many girls actually prefer the top bunk, you know," she said. "Look—Karen does."

For the first time, Natalie noticed that there was another girl in the bunk. She was hunched quietly over in the corner.

"Hey, Karen," Natalie said. "Where are you from?"

Karen spun around. "I'm from Chicago," she said.

Natalie blinked. "That's a long way away," she commented.

"My mother grew up in Pennsylvania, and she used to go to this camp for years and years," Karen said. "So that's why she sent me here. My plane got in really early this morning—I've been here forever."

Natalie nodded, taking Karen in. Natalie wasn't a snob, but she was pretty confident, and she made friends and could read people easily. A quick glance told her all she needed to know about Karen. The girl had thick brown hair pulled back into two braids going down either side of her head. Natalie knew lots of girls who wore their hair that way, but on Karen it really looked babyish, rather than cute. The hair, coupled with Karen's brown-and-green striped capri pants and a T-shirt that said LAKEVIEW ATHLETICS suggested that Karen was weird. Natalie's heart instantly went out to her. "Well, it's good that you had time to settle in before things got really crazy," Natalie told her.

Karen just shrugged and dove back into her trunk, leaving Natalie feeling a little bit foolish. She'd only been trying to be friendly, after all. It wasn't her fault Karen was odd. Also, if she'd been here all day, why was she still unpacking? Bizarre.

Stranger yet was when Karen re-emerged from

inside of her trunk with three stuffed animals. *Teddy bears?* Natalie thought incredulously. "Cool bears," she offered, trying again to keep an open mind.

Karen nodded coolly. "The rest are in my duffel."

The rest? Natalie thought. *Yikes.*

Natalie crossed over to the cubby wall and looked around again. Before she could even take a breath, though, Julie's bright, blond face was close to her own. "You can pick any cubby that you like!" Julie asserted, sounding like she thought this was a huge source of comfort to Natalie.

Four weeks, Natalie thought. It would only be four weeks until Visiting Day. Then her mother would come up, see the horror of Natalie's surroundings, and bust her out of Lakeview once and for all. There was no way her mother could be immune to things like moldy shower stalls and spiders on the toilet seats, right?

Was there?

chapter

THREE

"Can somebody *please* get the door for me? Ugh, I think I broke a nail!"

Natalie was sitting on the edge of her bed, actually hard at work filing her own nails, when she overheard the cry for help. She had finished unpacking over an hour ago, and had witnessed each new bunkmate walk in. There were only two more left to arrive, and the suspense was killing her. Glad to have something to do, Natalie sprung up and raced to be of help.

She threw the door open to be greeted with the sight of a very pretty older girl. "Hi, I'm Marissa, your CIT," the girl said, green eyes wide. "Thanks for opening the door." She sounded slightly out of breath, and she was balancing a bright pink milk crate overflowing with tons of cool stuff: a metallic blue iPod, a pair of fuzzy purple slippers, a hot pink clip-on lamp . . . Natalie's eyes flickered over the goods, appraising what Marissa had thought to bring. She'd have killed for the purple slippers, now that she saw the floor of the bunk.

"I'm Natalie," Natalie said. "And you probably want to get by." She stepped aside to let Marissa in. Marissa rushed in and immediately dropped her things on the floor next to the unclaimed single, then turned to embrace Julie.

"I'm so glad we get to work together!" Julie squealed, running her fingers through Marissa's wavy, light brown hair. "And I cannot *believe* how long your hair got!"

"You cut yours!" Marissa giggled.

"I did, too," a bold voice interrupted.

Natalie rolled her eyes. After just a few hours in the bunk, she already knew that voice all too well. It was Alex Kim. Alex had arrived just a few minutes after Natalie and had instantly made herself at home. It wasn't that she was so awful, really, just that . . . well, she was a Camp Lakeview regular. This was, like, her fifth summer or something. She knew all the ropes and was definite model-camper material, which made Natalie feel a little weird. Back in New York City, after all, *she* was the one who knew everyone, was friends with everyone, was the center of a million different groups of people. But obviously things would be different at Lakeview. For one, Marissa and Alex were embracing like long-lost relatives on a daytime soap opera.

"It looks great!" Marissa gushed, stepping back to admire Alex's straight black hair. Natalie herself thought the haircut was a little basic, but she supposed it suited Alex.

"Yeah, I needed to cut it to get it out of my face during soccer," Alex said, "but I like it so much that I'm probably not going to grow it back."

"No, short hair's great," Marissa said. "Now we can put all sorts of cool clips and stuff in it. And if you're feeling bold, we can even use some eye makeup, once your hair is pulled off your face."

Alex grimaced. "Gunk around my eyes? No, thanks."

Natalie smiled to herself, thinking of her own makeup kit stashed under her bed. At least that was one thing that she and Marissa could share.

"Are you into makeup?" Alex asked, turning toward Natalie. She was so direct that she somehow made it sound like an accusation.

"Um, yeah, I am," Natalie said, somewhat taken aback. She felt like she was expected to apologize for it or something.

Alex took a long look at Natalie, checking her out. Natalie bristled unintentionally. Who did this girl think she was? Just because she had been here a few summers in a row? That wasn't so special, in Natalie's opinion.

Well, Natalie knew at least one other girl here, and right now, she was especially glad for that. "Hey, Alyssa," she called out in the direction of the ceiling. Alyssa had shown up just after Natalie (the two of them having been on the same bus, and all), and had taken a cool fifteen minutes to put her things away before diving onto the bunk on top of Natalie's (it seemed like Julie had been right about the whole top bunk thing. Alex and Alyssa had swapped almost instantly). Alyssa had been there ever since. Natalie was into her and her whole low-key approach to camp. Alyssa seemed like the type of girl who hardly ever got bothered by anything.

"Yeah?" Alyssa called from her perch on her bed.

"Wanna go outside and play cards until the cookout? I will totally kick your butt at rummy 500."

There was a pause during which Natalie wondered if she'd somehow said the wrong thing. Maybe artsy, sensitive girls didn't like to play cards? Then, finally, "Yeah, right," and the sound of a ballpoint pen being capped. Natalie almost couldn't believe she'd succeeded in tearing Alyssa away from her notebook.

"We're leaving for the cookout in an hour!" Julie called as the girls left the bunk. "Don't go far!"

Natalie wasn't planning on going far, of course. But the stuffy bunk and everyone's unpacking was starting to make her uncomfortable. And for the first time since she'd arrived at Lakeview, Natalie felt like she could use some fresh air.

▲ ▲ ▲

"So, you're new, huh?" Natalie prodded as Alyssa shuffled the deck. They had settled in a grassy patch just outside the bunk and were waiting for the last two campers in 3C to arrive. Natalie had a sinking feeling that once they were all present and accounted for, there'd be icebreakers and more rounds of endless introductions. She was thankful to have a few moments, at least, outside and away from the chaos.

"Uh-huh," Alyssa nodded. "For the past two summers, I've been doing these drawing classes at a college in Middletown—that's right near where I live."

"In Pennsylvania?" Natalie asked.

"Nope, it's Jersey. Way in the south. Anyway, there's nothing special about the school, but, you know, I like to draw, so that was a pretty cool way to spend the summer."

"Why'd you come here?" Natalie wanted to know. Alyssa didn't seem like any more of a camp person than Natalie was.

Alyssa made a face and pushed her long dark hair off her shoulders. "You know. Parents. They decided I need to be more 'social.' " She made air quotes with her fingers and wrinkled her nose.

Natalie laughed. "I know what you mean. My mother told me that camp would help me build character. I told her I already have enough character."

"Totally. And you know"—Alyssa paused conspiratorially—"I bet Alex has enough character for the three of us combined." She winked to take the edge off her words. "Anyway, my mother wouldn't budge. I even tried to sic my dad on her, but he wasn't biting." Alyssa dealt the cards out. "What about yours?"

"What about my what?" Natalie asked, pretending not to get the question. She wasn't prepared to talk about her father just yet.

"Your dad," Alyssa said slowly, as though Natalie were a five-year-old. "Did he think you need more character, too?"

Natalie shrugged. "My dad's not really in the picture," she said simply, hoping that Alyssa would let the subject drop.

Alyssa flipped over the first card of the deck. "Ace of spades." She raised an eyebrow in Natalie's direction.

If she was wondering about Natalie's father, she didn't ask.

⛺ ⛺ ⛺

"My name is Grace, and I like gummy bears," Grace said, giggling. She gestured to the girl sitting beside her, Indian-style. "This is Chelsea and she likes cheesy music, and that's Alyssa and she likes art class. And Candace likes card games and Jenna likes jewelry." She paused, frowning in concentration. "Alex likes athletics." She exhaled.

Natalie and Alyssa hadn't gotten very far in their game before they had been called back in. The last two girls had arrived and it was time to do the "get-to-know-one-another" thing before dinner. Natalie's suspicion about icebreakers had turned out to be dead-on, and now she and her bunkmates were seated on the floor of the bunk, each offering one piece of information about herself and then forced to recite the names and details provided by the others before her. Based on where in the circle the game had begun, Natalie counted that she would be responsible for remembering every girl but two.

Natalie had a terrible memory.

"I'm Brynn," said the girl seated to Grace's left. Brynn had very short, very dark red hair and very pale skin. Her eyes were a bright, twinkly green. She had been one of the last two girls to show up, and it turned out she was best friends with Alex. They had even requested to bunk together, and they'd been inseparable since Brynn had arrived. Well, nearly inseparable, anyway—at least they weren't sitting next to each other in the circle.

Brynn had a very loud voice for such a small girl.

She wanted to be an actress, she explained, and was planning to spend most of her summer in the drama shack. Natalie had to admit that Brynn seemed very dramatic, so maybe that was a good thing. "I'm Brynn and I like Broadway shows. Grace likes gummy bears—so do I, Grace"—she beamed—"and Chelsea likes cheesy music and Alyssa likes art class and Jenna likes jewelry. Candace likes card games. And Alex likes athletics," Brynn said, flashing a blinding grin at her friend.

The bunk erupted in applause. Brynn hadn't faltered on a single name or detail. Even Natalie had to admit that she was slightly impressed. She took a moment to survey the circle of strange faces once more. In addition to the names that Brynn had just rattled off, she had also met Sarah, a friend of Alex and Brynn's and another big-time jock who was very into running (Natalie couldn't understand why anyone would be into running. What was the rush, anyway?), Karen, of course, the strange and youngish girl who'd been there all morning and had arrived with a collection of stuffed animals so large that it almost concerned Natalie, and Valerie, whose dark skin and cornrows reminded Natalie of Hannah from back home. Finally, there was Jessica, who wore her long, light brown hair in a sloppy bun on the top of her head and refused to answer to anything other than "Jessie."

The circle grew quiet, and Natalie realized that everyone was looking at her. *Right, my turn.* She took a deep breath and exhaled loudly. "My name is Natalie and I like . . . new experiences," she said, cringing inwardly at how corny the words sounded coming from her lips. Apparently, it was the right thing to say, though, because

Alyssa was giving her a sly grin and Julie was smiling away, full of encouragement.

Anyway, maybe if she tried hard enough, she could make herself believe it was true.

△ △ △

"Guys! We have extra hot dogs! I repeat, we have extra hot dogs!"

Natalie couldn't help but laugh to hear Pete shouting to be heard over the noise. *Good luck,* she thought. The entire camp had turned out for the cookout that evening, and campers were seated in clusters across the lawn, breaking off into countless individual conversations. Seeing everyone seated and enthusiastically eating, Natalie felt overwhelmed all over again. There were more campers at Lakeview than there were students in her entire school! Suddenly, Natalie was wondering if she was as social of a person as she had originally thought.

No, don't think that way, she scolded herself. *You're just freaking out because everything is strange and new. But it won't be this way forever. What would Hannah say if she could talk to you?* She knew what Hannah would say: "Chill out, girl—like it or not, you're at camp for the summer, so you may as well relax and make the best of it." Hannah was totally practical and levelheaded that way. It was so annoying.

And anyway, it wasn't as though Natalie was off in a corner by herself. She and Alyssa had squatted down in a circle with the rest of bunk 3C. Alex and Jenna were big on bunk unity. It was easy to see why they would both be favorites of any counselor.

Natalie felt a finger in her ribs and turned to find

Alyssa poking her. "Sure you don't want another hot dog?" The corners of her mouth were turned up in an impish grin.

"Ugh, I don't even want to think about what the first one did to me," Natalie protested. "There must be something wrong with them. You were smart to stick to the side salads." She waved her paper plate in the direction of a group of boys who had jumped up and made a mad dash for the barbecue pit the minute Pete announced second helpings.

"Oh, my brother and his friends'll eat anything," Jenna said. "It's so gross."

"Which one's your brother?" Natalie asked.

"Well, the one who's standing on line like he hasn't eaten in weeks—*so* not true, by the way—is Adam. He's my twin and he's in 3F. So you'll meet him when we have electives and stuff. My sister Stephanie is a CIT. She's good friends with Marissa so you'll meet her soon, I'm sure."

"Oh, we have electives with the boys?" Natalie asked. Suddenly, camp was sounding just a little more interesting.

Jenna shuddered. "Unfortunately. For most of the day, you travel with your bunk to different activities, but twice a day you get to go to your electives, and those are a mix of everyone in our age division. Oh, and they have swim sessions and meals with us, too. We're gonna have to stick together if we want to avoid getting splashed. Although," Jenna leaned in, a mischievous look on her face, "I'm usually pretty good at pulling pranks on them and stuff. They never know what hit 'em."

Natalie nodded. "Good to know." At this point,

she was more interested in scoping out the boys than in playing pranks on them. Was that going to be just one more thing that set her apart from her bunkmates? She pushed herself up from the ground and dusted any stray grass off her legs. Nature was turning out to be very . . . well, messy. "I'm gonna toss my trash. Does anyone have anything for me to throw out?" she offered. Jenna and Alyssa shook their heads no.

Natalie fought her way through a swarm of nasty-looking insects and gingerly tossed her plate and utensils into the garbage can. A bit of mayonnaise splashed up onto her arm, making her a prime target of the insects' interest. "Oh, ick," she grumbled, and wandered toward the barbecue table to grab a napkin to clean herself up.

"Look, he *said* there are a ton of hot dogs left."

"But, um, I still have my hamburger, Chelsea."

Natalie turned to see Chelsea and Karen standing next to the barbecue table, apparently in the midst of some serious negotiations. It was plain to see that Karen definitely did have an entire hamburger sitting untouched on her plate. Which Chelsea definitely had designs on. Natalie watched the exchange with curiosity.

"Come on, Karen, I'm starving. And I'm allergic to hot dogs. Don't you want to do me a favor?" Chelsea pressed.

"Well, but . . . I mean . . . how can you be allergic to hot dogs? Or, I mean, if you're allergic to hot dogs, then wouldn't you also be allergic to hamburgers?"

"Well, okay," Chelsea said, quickly backtracking, "I'm not exactly allergic. But it's, like, I really don't like them and they really make me sick. Ever since I was little. Anyway," she continued, "my mother is going to send me up a care package next week, and I can totally hook you up. I mean, wouldn't you want a pack of Twizzlers or something? That's fair, right?"

Karen looked unconvinced, but she was obviously afraid to stand up to Chelsea. "Um, I guess," she said. "Yeah, fine." She pushed her plate at Chelsea and walked away, her head down.

"Wait a minute!" Chelsea called after her, smiling like the cat that had swallowed the canary. "Don't you even want to get a hot dog?"

Karen rushed off, not bothering to answer. Natalie observed the entire exchange silently, thinking. She didn't like what she had just seen. Was Chelsea some kind of bully?

"Where'd you go? We thought you'd, like, fallen into the garbage can or something," Grace teased when Natalie had made her way back to the bunk. "Or were you having a little last-minute hot-dog-eating contest?"

Before Natalie could answer, she was interrupted by the sound of hoots, whistles, and feet stamping on the ground. She glanced over and saw that Alex and Jenna were the cause of the commotion. They were hissing and booing at a group of girls walking by.

"What's the sitch?" Natalie asked, turning to Grace, who had also joined in on the shrieking and hollering.

"It's bunk 3A," Grace explained between whistles. "They're our rivals."

"Based on what?" Natalie asked.

"Oh, gosh, I don't even remember anymore. They've played all kinds of jokes on us over the last few summers. Somehow, it just developed. I mean, it's all in good fun. You'll see—just don't leave your toothbrush out at night, is all I'm saying," she warned.

Natalie didn't like the sound of that one bit. *All in good fun? Really?* she wondered.

When was the fun going to start, then?

chapter
FOUR

Within five minutes of first waking up, Natalie immediately noticed two things. The first was that it was about thirty degrees below zero in the bunk, and her cute little sleep shorts were really not doing the trick of keeping her warm. She remembered that Julie had tried to warn her the night before of how cold it could get in the mountains, but for some reason, she hadn't let herself believe it. *Note to self,* she thought, thrusting her hands underneath the covers and rubbing them vigorously across her bare legs in the hopes of warming them up, *for future reference: Julie knows stuff.*

The second thing Natalie noticed—and this was going to be an even bigger problem, she decided—was the horrible trumpet blaring through the open windows. *We couldn't have just set an alarm clock?* she wondered.

Okay, so she wasn't a morning person.

From across the room, someone groaned. "For Pete's sake, *please* make that noise stop!" It was Grace. She clearly wasn't a morning person, either.

"What time is it, even?" Natalie demanded. She had worn her cute pink waterproof sports watch to bed (at last, she'd finally have a chance to make use of all of its "outdoor" settings), but she had no intention of taking her hands out from underneath her blanket to check.

"It's quarter of," Julie said brightly, bouncing across the room. She looked as freshly scrubbed and perky as ever. Natalie suspected she even looked that way in her sleep.

"Quarter of *what*?" Natalie pressed. "I don't believe in getting up before the sevens."

"Well, my dear, I'm sorry to have to break it to you, but if that's the case, then you're going to have to stay in bed for another fifteen minutes. But that would only leave you fifteen minutes to get dressed. Your call."

Natalie flew up in bed. "We have *half an hour* to be ready for breakfast?"

She looked around the bunk. To every side she could see girls rummaging through their cubbies in various stages of dress. Karen was sitting on the edge of her bed holding a sock up in front of her face, looking confused.

"But, Julie," Natalie said, careful to keep the edge she was feeling from creeping into her tone, "it takes me at least twenty minutes to shower."

"Well, then you'd better hurry, Natalie. And tomorrow morning, you'll just have to try to get up before the bugle. Does your watch have an alarm?" Julie asked. She didn't sound unsympathetic, just matter-of-fact. But that didn't make Natalie feel any better.

"Well, I guess I can rush," Natalie said. "Whatever. I can do makeup when we get back from breakfast."

"I'm sorry, Nat, but after breakfast we really only have a half an hour or so, and that's for our bunk chores," Julie said. "But you don't need makeup to look gorgeous!"

Speak for yourself, Natalie thought glumly, hoisting herself reluctantly out of bed, stepping into her flip-flops, and padding off into the bathroom.

As she shuffled into a shower stall, she was nearly mowed over by Alex, who was running a comb through her wet hair. *Of course*, Natalie thought. It only fit that Alex had woken up on time to shower. She was, like, Supercamper.

Natalie stepped into a stall and turned the hot water on full blast. She ducked under the stream—and let out a startled shriek.

"What is it?" Julie asked, rushing in.

"It's FREEZING!" Natalie shouted. The water was about as cold as the morning air in the bunk had been. Also, a huge clump of wiry hair was poking its way out of the drain. *Gross*.

"Sorry," said a voice from the direction of the sinks. "I might have used up the hot water." It was Chelsea.

"Are you *allergic* to cold water?" Natalie mumbled sarcastically, surprising herself. She hadn't meant to be nasty, it had just slipped out.

"Did you say something?" Chelsea asked.

"No, I didn't say anything," Natalie replied quickly, covering. "I didn't say anything at all."

She ducked back underneath the cold water, resigned to her fate for this morning, at least.

▲ ▲ ▲

If Marissa had been around in the morning, she probably would have been able to give Natalie some "quick tips to getting gorgeous FAST." After all, she had about a million magazines strewn on top of her bed, and that was the gist of most of the headlines Natalie had seen. But Marissa was long gone by the time the girls of 3C had woken up. Julie explained that it was because as a CIT, Marissa had to work as a waitress in the mess hall. So she had to get there early to set up for the morning meal.

Walking to the mess hall, Natalie was actually kind of excited to see Marissa waiting on them. She wondered if all the CITs had cute matching uniforms that they wore when they served. And maybe Marissa would carry a funny notepad in her apron that she would use for taking orders, like in a real restaurant. Natalie wondered what they normally had for breakfast at Lakeview. If the cookout was any indication, the food wouldn't be any great shakes, but that was no big deal. She could live on scrambled eggs if she had to.

"Oh, and if the bug juice is yellow, don't drink it," Alex was saying to a group of girls.

"Um, why?" Karen asked quietly. By now Natalie had gotten used to the fact that Karen did everything quietly.

"Because you don't know what they put in it," Alex explained. "I mean, I guess you never can be too sure, but with yellow, it's like asking for trouble. I wouldn't put it past them if they peed in it," she said, lowering her voice.

"*Ew*," Karen said.

"That *can't* be true," Natalie interjected, holding out hope that Alex was just being dramatic.

Jenna nodded solemnly. "It is, though. My oldest brother Matt—he's not here anymore, he's really old, and this summer he's going to a summer college program in science, how boring is *that?*—anyway, his friend used to work in the kitchen. You would not *believe* the stuff that goes on in there. I mean, pee in the bug juice is seriously the least of it. I can tell you stories—"

"—Please don't," Natalie begged.

"Okay, okay," Alex said, breaking into the conversation again like a weary referee. "Let's just put it this way—if we tell you to avoid something, you'll just have to trust us."

"Fair enough," Natalie said.

▲ ▲ ▲

"This is our table!" Julie shouted, beckoning the girls to a long, cafeteria-style table and bench set just inside the mess hall.

They'd been inside the mess hall for all of three seconds, and already Natalie's head was spinning. For starters, the room was enormous, cavernous, with soaring ceilings held in place with long wooden beams and rafters. Which of course made for the kind of acoustics that sent the racket of at least two hundred separate conversations up into the air only to pour loudly back down. Natalie shook her head. So far, everything about camp seemed to be chaotic. Certainly the paint-splattered banners dangling from the walls, hailing color wars of years gone by. Natalie wasn't sure yet what color war was, and she was almost afraid to ask. It sounded potentially stressful. And there was the clatter of silverware clinking against the surface of the tables. And the laughter coming from her own fellow bunkmates. Was she honestly the only person here who didn't find camp to be one great big party?

She looked up to see Alyssa cradling her chin on her palm, looking thoughtful. Okay, so she wasn't exactly the only one. But that didn't make it much better. Natalie was still hoping that her mother would come up on Visiting Day, take one look at this place, and throw Natalie into the backseat of her SUV and never look back. But Visiting Day was four long weeks away. And Natalie couldn't bear the thought of having to mope her way through each passing day. There had to be some way to make the situation better, more bearable, at least.

Didn't there?

A platter of rubbery-looking blackened pucks landed on the table in front of her with an unceremonious thud. Natalie gazed intently at the dish. "Nope, nuh-uh," she decided, looking at Alex questioningly. "Not a clue."

Alex leaned forward and put her face closer to the food. The gesture did nothing to encourage Natalie to try the food. She inhaled deeply—*it's always nice when someone breathes directly on your food*, Natalie thought fleetingly—and wrinkled her forehead in concentration.

"French toast," she pronounced, pushing the tray toward Natalie. "It's all yours."

Natalie regarded the dried-up slabs of bread again. In no way did they resemble French toast. French toast was what she ordered at her local diner on Sundays, when she and her mother had brunch. French toast was thick and eggy and covered in toasted pecans. It looked nothing like a hockey puck. And it wasn't black. "Oh, I couldn't," Natalie said shortly. "Really."

"Come on, Nat, you have to eat something," Julie prodded. "Here comes Marissa. Maybe she can tell you what else there is for breakfast."

Natalie glanced up. It didn't seem as though Marissa had paid too much attention to any beauty tips this morning. She was wearing a very un-hip plastic apron over cutoff shorts and a tank top, and she had a smudge of something yellow—possibly egg yolk— drying across her cheek. Her eyes looked red and tired, and her hair hung limply at her shoulders. Natalie got the distinct impression that there weren't too many alternatives to the morning menu. Marissa certainly wasn't carrying pen and paper, anyway.

"What's wrong?" Marissa added, sounding harried. "Do you guys need more food?"

"No—no!" Alex said quickly. "I mean, we're fine, we're all good," she corrected.

Natalie could see that working as a waitress was very hard work, and the last thing she wanted to do was add to Marissa's burden. But the French toast was seriously out of the question. "Marissa," she began slowly, "is there, ah, anything else to eat?"

For a moment, Marissa looked as though she wanted to cry. Then she brightened. "I think there's fruit!" she said, darting off in the direction of the kitchen. Natalie's spirits soared. She'd be able to at least make it through the morning on a banana. Lunch *had* to be better than this disaster.

"Here you go," Marissa pronounced, depositing a cracked plastic bowl in the middle of the table. Natalie reached in and grabbed an apple. Her finger immediately sunk through the skin and into a mealy bruise.

"Um, thanks," she said, sighing. "Do you know what's for lunch?"

▲ ▲ ▲

After the girls had finished eating—or, in Natalie's case, pushing food around on her plate in the hopes that Julie would *think* she was eating—they filed out of the mess hall so that Marissa and the other CITs would be able to clean up. If Marissa was going to be spending so much time in the kitchen, Natalie fretted, she'd never have any energy leftover for the bunk. And then who was going to help her when she flat-ironed her hair? Alyssa was cool, but she didn't seem like the kind of girl who spent a whole lot of time on her hair, after all.

Natalie was so completely lost in her thoughts that she didn't even notice that she had stomped directly into someone. A boy someone, to be specific. The boy someone grunted and stepped forward forcefully. Her foot caught on the back of his shoe and practically pulled it off his foot.

"Hey, what's your problem?" the boy asked, whirling around. He sounded annoyed.

"It wasn't on purpose," Natalie said, feeling defensive. So she was a klutz. Whatever. Just one more reason why she wasn't going to win Camper of the Week.

But one look at her victim, and Natalie felt like maybe there would be some upsides to spending the summer at Lakeview, after all.

The boy, whoever he was, peered at her curiously. He had thick, curly black hair and eyes so deeply blue that it took Natalie a moment to figure out what color they were. Somewhere in the back of her mind, she realized she was staring, but she couldn't help it. It didn't matter, anyway, because whoever he was, he was staring right back at her.

Then one of his bunkmates jostled into him, and the moment was broken. He reached down and coaxed his foot back into his sneaker, stood up, stretched his arms over his head, and walked out of the mess hall without another glance in Natalie's direction.

"His name is Simon," said a voice in Natalie's ear.

"Huh?" Natalie asked, spinning to see Marissa standing just beside her, looking exhausted but eagerly taking in the scene. "Who?" she asked again, trying to sound casual.

Marissa shot her a knowing look. She waved her hand toward Simon's retreating frame. "His name is Simon. He's in bunk 3F."

Natalie shrugged. "Whatever," she said, feeling color rush to her cheeks. She gathered her composure and nodded toward the exit, where Julie and the rest of 3C were making their way out of the building. "I have to, uh, catch up," she said, and took off before Marissa could say anything else.

Simon. Okay. So he had cool eyes. But so what? What did she care about Simon?

FIVE

The next morning, the girls returned to their bunk after breakfast. By now, Natalie had had a chance to see that Julie hadn't been exaggerating yesterday—there really *wasn't* any time to do any last-minute primping—not that there was any reason to, in this humidity. The morning chill had gradually warmed over, and already little trickles of sweat were forming on the insides of Natalie's elbows and the backs of her knees. She could only imagine what the weather would be like by midday.

For now, though, the girls were responsible for doing chores. Back home, Natalie's mother worked such long hours at her art gallery that she had hired a housekeeper to come in once a week to clean. Natalie often straightened up her room—at least, she made her bed every morning and emptied out the dishwasher when necessary—but that was about the extent of her acquaintance with chores. Julie proudly held up the chore wheel that she had created. On the inner circle of the wheel, she had written up all the tasks, such as scrubbing out the toilets, emptying the wastebaskets, or sweeping the front porch. On the outer circle were all the girls' names. Every day, Julie would shift the outer wheel, so that each day the girls would rotate which chores they were responsible for. "I can't wait until it's my turn to do toilets," Grace quipped as she headed outside with the trash.

"Girls, before you start your chores, listen up. I want to give you your schedules, okay?" Julie called out. "Every day after breakfast, we come back to the bunk and clean for a half an hour. Then after that, we've got a specialty that we travel to as a bunk: nature, arts and crafts, ceramics, woodworking, drama, photography, and the newspaper. It switches every day. After that comes instructional swim. Today you'll be taking your swim tests for placement. After swim comes a free choice, then sports, then lunch, second free choice, then siesta after free swim. While you do your chores, I'll be talking to each of you individually and taking down your selections for your free choices. You should pick three, and I promise I'll do my best to make sure that you get two of the ones that you pick. Okay? Get to it! Karen, come talk to me about free choice."

Dutifully (and, truth be told, somewhat eagerly), Karen put down her scrub brush and scampered over to Julie's bunk. She didn't seem very sorry about having to put off bathroom duty.

As she swept the front porch, Natalie thought about which free choices would be most interesting to her. Photography could be really cool—definitely something she could keep up back in the city if it turned out that she was any good at it. So she would choose that. And secondly, she wouldn't mind writing for the newspaper. Her English teacher in school was always telling her she was a good writer. And for a third choice she would pick drama. Drama was something else that she would probably be good at. After all, it ran in the family. Which was, of course, one of the reasons why she usually steered clear of it. But if it came down to drama or nature, she'd take drama all the way. It was definitely better than any of the other, "campier" choices available. What *was* woodworking, anyway?

Natalie brushed all the excess dust off the porch and directly onto the ground. Julie hadn't given her a dust pan and, besides, the ground was nothing but dirt, anyway. She picked her broom up and walked back inside the bunk.

Inside, though, she was immediately given the shock of her life. Over Alex's bed was a huge poster of Tad Maxwell from his latest movie, *Spy in the Big City*. Instantly, Natalie's blood ran cold. What was that poster doing up? Was Alex a fan of the "spy" movies? Did she know who Tad Maxwell *really* was? No, Natalie decided, she couldn't know. It had to be some sort of coincidence. And if Natalie could keep her cool, Alex would *never* know, either.

She willed herself to maintain her composure. "Hey, Alex, is that your poster?" she asked as casually as she could.

"Huh? Oh, yeah," Alex said, tossing a wet sponge into a bucket of soapy water. She had been working on the sinks in the bathroom. "Isn't it cool? My older brother loves Tad Maxwell 'cause he kicks so much butt, and then he got me into the 'spy' movies. I'm a *huge* fan. I think he's really cute, too. What about you?"

"Oh, um, you know. I think Tad Maxwell is cool,"

Natalie stammered, "but there are, you know, lots of other things I like better. I'm more into chick flicks," she said, pulling herself together.

"Yeah, me too!" Grace said, coming up behind her. "And musicals. Does it get any better than *Grease*?" She broke into a few bars of "Summer Nights," causing all the girls to crack up.

"Nat, you're the only one who hasn't chosen her electives yet," Julie said, interrupting the laughter. "Do you know what you want?"

"Yeah," Natalie said, crossing the room to squat on the floor next to Julie's bed. "Anything but nature! Seriously, though," she continued, "I'd be into photography, the newspaper, and . . . drama. Yeah, drama could be cool," she finished, sounding slightly uncertain. She glanced at Alex's poster again.

Natalie thought maybe she already had enough drama in her life.

▲ ▲ ▲

Julie worked on putting together the girls' free-choice schedules while they were in arts and crafts. Natalie and her bunkmates were hard at work twisting long plastic strands into specially woven patterns. "What are these things for, anyway?" Natalie whispered to Jenna. She was used to being really good at things when she wanted to be, but at camp, everything was different and unfamiliar. She felt really frustrated.

Jenna shrugged. "It's lanyard. It's a camp tradition. You'll have about a million lanyard key chains by the time the summer is over."

Natalie thought about the cool lip-gloss key chain that Hannah had given her at her last birthday. That was way more useful than this . . . *lanyard*. But she had promised herself that she would give camp a try, so she kept her opinion to herself. And, anyway, the pink and turquoise color scheme she'd thought up was looking pretty good, in her opinion. Way tropical.

"Okay, girls, I've got your schedules worked out," Julie announced as the girls worked. "Now, I want you all to know that I did everything I could to make sure that you each got at least one of your three choices, and I'm pretty sure I was successful. But if you're not totally happy with your free choices, just know that we swap every two weeks, okay? So you won't be spending two full months doing something you're not that into. But try to keep an open mind you might find you're better at something than you would have expected." With that, she called the girls over to a corner of the art room one at a time to let them know their schedules.

Natalie watched in anticipation as one by one, the girls were given their choices. Grace skipped back to the art table after talking to Julie. "Ceramics and drama," she said, beaming. "So awesome. I wanted to be in the school play, and I wanted to learn to use the kiln. Last year, Alex made a really cool coffee mug, and I want to do the same thing."

Brynn was also thrilled with her choices. "Drama," she practically sang. "I heard that the play this year is going to be *Peter Pan*, and I think I'd be the perfect choice for Wendy. And also the newspaper," she said as an afterthought. She began to hum the chorus to one of the songs from *Peter Pan* under her breath. Natalie could see that Brynn already had visions of her name up in lights.

"Natalie?" Julie called.

Natalie pushed her lanyard aside and jumped up. She rushed over to Julie, wishing she didn't feel so nervous. *It's just free choice, Nat,* she reminded herself. "What'd I get?" she asked breathlessly.

"Well, you've got the newspaper for first free," Julie said. "With Alyssa. I thought you two would like to be together."

Natalie exhaled sharply. "Great. That could be fun."

"But," Julie said, looking slightly uncomfortable, "there were just too many overlaps for most of the rest of the choices, so I had to give you something different than what you asked for."

Natalie bristled. "What'd I get?" she asked, a sense of dread coming over her.

"Keep in mind it's just for two weeks, and you never know what you might learn," Julie said, stalling for time and burying her face in her clipboard.

Now Natalie was really starting to feel anxious. "Julie," she pressed, "come on."

"Well, for second free, you've got nature," Julie said.

"What?" Natalie cried. "Julie, no way!"

"I promise, Nat, it's the only way I could make it work. I swear. And it's only for two weeks."

"Two weeks is a long time!" Natalie insisted. "Julie, I'm pretty sure I'm allergic to nature. I mean, I'm from New York City!"

"Don't be silly," Julie protested. "The truth is, Nat,"

she said, lowering her voice, "I'm starting to get to know you girls, and I can tell that you're strong. You're a confident chick. And if I stick you in nature, you're gonna do well—even if it's not your first choice. Now, I can't say that about everyone in the bunk. So I need you to be the strong one, and to suck it up and try something new and different. Just think of it as taking one for the team. Can you do that for me?" Julie fixed her bright blue eyes on Natalie, and suddenly Natalie found it hard to say no.

"When you put it that way," Natalie said, rolling her eyes, "how can I argue?"

Julie threw her arms around Natalie. "I knew I could count on you, Natalie! I totally owe you!" she exclaimed.

"Yes," Natalie agreed solemnly. "Yes, you do."

"Oh, you got nature, too?" Chelsea asked, passing by. She didn't sound very sympathetic.

"Uh, yeah. Does that mean you got nature?" Natalie asked.

Chelsea tossed her sun-streaked blond hair over her shoulders. "Yup. But you know, it's different for me. I'm from the country. So I'll be able to identify the poison ivy and stuff—and avoid it," she said snidely. She shot Natalie a self-satisfied grin and stalked off.

Natalie turned back to Julie again, a fresh wave of panic washing over her.

"Nat, she's just kidding. Ha ha," Julie said pleadingly.

Marissa, back from kitchen duty, came up behind Natalie and rubbed her shoulders. "Just think of it as building character," she said.

Great. More character, Natalie thought. *At what point*

do we decide that I've got enough character? She sighed. "I'll be a good sport," she said, resigned. "But in that case, have I mentioned how much you owe me?" she asked again.

▲ ▲ ▲

"Nat, relax. Chelsea was just being . . . Chelsea. Poison ivy is really easy to identify," Valerie said as the two trudged over to the nature shack. "Besides, I seriously doubt that the nature counselor is going to send us off into a patch of it." She giggled and shook her head, making the beads in her cornrows clink. "I bet you anything we spend today playing with the rabbits or whatever."

"Rabbits?" Natalie asked nervously. "I think I really *am* allergic to rabbits."

Valerie raised an eyebrow at her. "Come on."

"Well, I mean, I've never, like, been tested for it or anything, but who knows? I mean, I *could* be," Natalie said defensively.

"Why don't we wait and see?" Valerie suggested.

"We can wait and see, sure, but I'm telling you, Valerie, even if I'm not allergic to the rabbits or the guinea pigs or the skunks—"

"—Um, I really don't think they keep *skunks* inside the nature shack—" Valerie cut in.

"—*whatever*. The point is, that no matter if I turn out to be the world's biggest animal lover, I would want, you know, some cuddly kittens or something. I mean, there's no way on *Earth* that I'm going to suddenly be all into nature—" Natalie pushed the door open to the nature shack.

And then she stopped her tirade mid-sentence. Because there was one thing, she realized, that could just make nature bearable. One person, to be exact. One boy-person with denim blue eyes. Eyes that happened to be trained directly on her, making her suddenly self-conscious of how incredibly negative she must sound.

Simon.

Natalie stopped short as she walked into the room, causing Valerie to step directly into her and send her forward a few paces. "Ow," she said, barely taking note of the collision.

"God, Nat, stare much?" Chelsea mumbled. She had arrived a few minutes earlier and was already seated.

Natalie ignored Chelsea and went to take a seat at the table—not directly next to Simon, because that would be too obvious, but near enough that she could keep an eye on him during the session.

"Hello, guys, my name's Roseanne," said a woman standing at the front of the table. Roseanne looked like the type of person who would lead a class in nature, if there ever were such a thing: She was wiry, thin, and impossibly tall, with long, dark curly hair shooting off in every direction. She wore faded cargo shorts, a tank top, and broken-in hiking sandals. Natalie guessed Roseanne was probably a vegetarian. "Welcome to nature. In the nature shack—and outside, as well—we're going to learn all about our environment. But if you want to commune with nature, you're going to have to be responsible about it. And that means respecting nature and not disturbing or depleting it."

Scratch vegetarian, Natalie decided. *Vegan. Definite vegan.* Natalie herself had considered becoming a vegetarian, but had to drop it when she realized it meant giving up sushi.

"So first some rules that will help protect *you*," Roseanne continued. She picked up a big hand-lettered chart with some bright pictures of various plants glued onto it. "Does anyone know how to identify poison ivy?"

From her left, Natalie was dimly aware of Valerie stifling a snort and elbowing her in the ribs. But only dimly.

She was much more focused on Simon.

Natalie was walking away from the nature shack, eagerly contemplating which magazine from her mother's latest care package she was going to bring to free swim when she heard someone calling after her.

"So, ah, you're not too into nature."

Natalie turned to find Simon slightly out of breath, but walking casually next to her as though he had been there all along. "Well, I like *nature*, and all," she began, wanting to sound like she had a "positive attitude," "but, you know, it's just . . . okay, I hate nature," she finally conceded.

Simon broke out laughing. "Roseanne can freak you out a little, I know, with her 'avoid this plant,' and 'this thing is poisonous,' but the truth is you're not going to be rubbing up against any poison ivy or anything in the nature shack."

"What about poison oak?" Natalie quipped.

"Negative," Simon replied. "And the thing is that the animals are really cool."

"I guess," Natalie agreed reluctantly. "I'm much more into domesticated animals. Like hamsters. Cats. The occasional lapdog."

"Oh, that's right, you're from New York. I guess they don't really have big dogs in the city, because of all the apartments," Simon reasoned.

Natalie stared at him, puzzled. "How did you know I was from New York City?" she asked, frankly curious.

Simon colored. "I guess, um, someone mentioned it," he offered, shrugging. "I guess."

But Simon was looking *way* too embarrassed to have just found out about her hometown by accident, Natalie decided. Based on his guilty expression, he had definitely done some digging into her background. Not that she minded. *Interesting,* Natalie thought.

Very interesting indeed.

chapter
SIX

On Wednesday morning, Natalie woke with enough time to shower. She had somehow figured out how to drag herself out of her bed even amidst the morning chill so that she could get herself together before flag-raising. Maybe it was a survival instinct. After all, this *was* the wilderness, wasn't it?

Flag-raising was a particularly bizarre camp ritual, and even though she'd by now been at Lakeview for six whole days, Natalie still wasn't really getting the point of it. The process was straightforward: All the campers from all the divisions came to the field just in front of the flagpole every morning. This was located in front of the camp director's, Dr. Steve's, office. All the bunks in the divisions met together, along with their counselors and individual division heads. It was important to Dr. Steve that all of Lakeview "greet the day together."

Back in New York, Natalie and her mother liked to greet the day as slowly as possible, and usually with whole-wheat bagels and herbal tea, so this "stand at attention and salute" thing was a pretty big shock to her system.

As Natalie wrapped a towel around herself, she overheard a conversation from the stall next door.

"Are you going to wear your lavender headband?" she heard someone ask in a snotty tone. *Chelsea*, she thought. It had to be. Not that Natalie was a snoop, but suddenly the conversation was that much more interesting. She willed herself inanimate and undetectable.

"Uh, yeah, why?" It was Karen, sounding a little uncertain.

"Well, I was just thinking that it's a shame, because it sort of makes you look like a baby."

Natalie felt a pang of sympathy for Karen.

"Oh, um, do you think so?" Karen asked sadly.

"Totally. You shouldn't even bother—that is, unless you want everyone to think you're a complete *baby*," Chelsea repeated, taunting.

"You're probably right," Karen said. A pause followed, leading Natalie to think that Karen was taking the offending headband out right then and there.

"Much better," Chelsea said, confirming Natalie's thought. "But, you know, you *really* should brush your hair."

"Thanks, Chelsea," Karen said. It upset Natalie to hear the relief in Karen's voice. It certainly wasn't worth getting upset over Chelsea's opinion, annoying as she was!

"So, you know, Karen . . ." Chelsea continued.

Natalie's ears pricked up. Chelsea sounded just a tad *too* casual.

"Yeah?" Karen asked.

"So, now that you're not wearing that headband . . . I guess you wouldn't mind if I borrowed it?"

Natalie had to stop herself from gasping out loud. So Chelsea had manipulated the whole exchange, trying to make Karen feel bad about the headband, just because she wanted to wear it herself? That was just too, too mean.

Then again, she wasn't sure why she was so surprised. After all, it was typical Chelsea.

Natalie told Alyssa about the conversation she'd overheard on their way to the flag-raising. Alyssa agreed that Chelsea could be awful, but she didn't think it was really worth saying anything. "I mean, she didn't do anything to you, right?" Alyssa asked. "So, it's really not any of your business. Karen might even be upset if she found out you overheard. Like, embarrassed."

"You're probably right," Natalie agreed. "But what a pain Chelsea is."

Alyssa put a hand on Natalie's forearm, saying, "Let's not let her ruin our good time."

Natalie had to snicker. Standing in front of a flag-pole at daybreak in the freezing cold was definitely not what she considered a "good time"!

"Who's in charge of raising the flag today?" Natalie asked. A different bunk was responsible every morning.

"Three-A," Alex chimed in authoritatively. Just about *everything* Alex said or did was authoritative. She was nice enough, but sometimes her gung-ho attitude grated on Natalie. But she knew what her mother would say about that: *broader horizons, yadda yadda yadda* . . . So she just smiled at Alex and said, "Thanks."

Meredith Bergmont, a petite blonde who weighed, Natalie guessed, less than a hummingbird, stepped forward. She tugged on the rope-pulley mechanism that raised the flag. In fact, Stephanie was so focused on her job that she didn't even notice exactly what she was raising—the American flag, yes.

But that wasn't all.

Meredith finally put the rope down when the first wave of riotous laughter hit the air. She looked up to see all the divisions of Lakeview doubled over, clutching their stomachs with hysteria. Underneath the American flag was a banner that read: "WE SEE LONDON, WE SEE FRANCE. WE SEE 3A'S UNDERPANTS."

And after that?

Strung on the flagpole and waving proudly in the breeze were twelve pairs of girls' underwear. More specifically, the girls' of 3A's underwear.

Natalie's jaw dropped. "Oh my gosh! Who did that?" she demanded, turning to Alyssa. But Alyssa was laughing too hard to answer, pausing only to catch her breath and wipe tears from the corners of her eyes.

Looking around, Natalie could tell that Alyssa wasn't the only one having an extreme reaction. But to her left, three girls looked like they were enjoying the scene just a shade more than everyone else.

Jenna, Grace, and Brynn.

None of the counselors could prove anything, though, and the prank was harmless enough. And so once the panties had been lowered and safely returned to Lizzie, 3A's most embarrassed counselor, flag-raising pro-ceeded as though there had been no interruption at all.

▲ ▲ ▲

"So, today we're going to talk about interviews," Keith, the newspaper specialist said. Keith hadn't ever worked on an actual newspaper—just a small computer magazine published in South Jersey—but Natalie liked him just the same. He seemed very enthusiastic, and nothing about the newspaper office was potentially poisonous, alive, or otherwise natural. Therefore, Natalie had decided that newspaper was just about her favorite place to be at Lakeview. That is, when she wasn't back in the bunk reading magazines while Alyssa sketched. Keith continued, "An interview is a reporter's opportunity to talk to a famous figure or other celebrity, sure, but what people don't always realize is that the interview is also the reporter's opportunity to paint the subject in any light he or she sees fit. Many people assume that interviews they read are a reflection of the subject's true thoughts and words, but often, the interview is strongly influenced by the reporter's vision."

Natalie snorted almost without realizing. "I'll say," she muttered to herself.

Alyssa looked at her friend quizzically. "What do you mean?" she asked.

Natalie looked up to see that not only was Alyssa looking at her, but so were a few other campers. *Whoops,* she thought. She hadn't meant to actually say anything aloud. Now what was she going to do? "Uh, well, I just mean—I read a thing in *Teen People* last week that made Britney Spears look like a total moron. And I don't really think that she is," she stammered, covering.

"Yeah, I'm sure she's, like, a real brainiac," said Claudia, a girl from 3B that Natalie and Alyssa were starting to get to know.

"She's *way* smarter than Christina Aguilera," Natalie protested defensively, hoping to turn the conversation away from her little slip. "Don't you think, Alyssa?"

"Huh? Well, I guess . . . but she's nothing compared to, uh, Mindy Moore," Alyssa said.

Everyone at their table cracked up. Alyssa was so hopeless when it came to mainstream pop culture. That was one of the things Natalie liked best about her—she was into more original music, books, and movies than most of the kids Natalie knew—even her friends back in the city.

"*Mandy* Moore, Lyss," Claudia said, laughing hysterically. "*Mandy*"

Natalie giggled with her friends, and Alyssa did, too. Natalie was especially relieved for the change in conversation topic. But when Natalie glanced up at her friend, she caught Alyssa gazing at her with a strange expression.

Did her friend suspect that Natalie's comment meant more than she was letting on?

▲   ▲   ▲

"Pass it here! Alex, pass it here!"

Natalie looked up to see a soccer ball nearly glance off Chelsea's face. Naturally, the girl was completely undaunted. Chelsea may have been a total princess in the mornings, spending time blowing out her hair and picking just the right outfit, but when it came to sports, she was a big-time jock. Right now, for example, she dipped backward and deftly sidestepped the soccer ball as it shot toward her. Once it hit the ground, she leaped on top of it and began dribbling swiftly toward the opposite team's goal.

"Go! Go! Go!" Alex shouted, egging Chelsea on. Brynn stood beside Alex, screaming wildly and waving her arms in the air in a wordless show of support.

"Do you think we're supposed to be going after her?" Natalie whispered to Alyssa, who was also hanging out in the far left field. Natalie was fast learning that in addition to nature, there were several other aspects of camp that weren't exactly her strong suit. Sports being one of them.

Alyssa shrugged. "Not sure. What does 'defense?' mean, anyway?"

Natalie grinned. She and Alyssa really were on the same page.

Suddenly, the players on the field—all the rest of the girls in bunk 3C—erupted into a mixture of triumphant battle cries and booing and hissing. Obviously, Chelsea had scored. No surprise there.

Brian, the head of sports, blew his whistle shrilly, bringing the game to a formal conclusion. "Nice work, girls!" he shouted in his thick Australian accent. "Chelsea, great goal! Alex, awesome assist!"

"I personally think we did some mighty fine standing around," Natalie mumbled to Alyssa under her breath.

Alyssa stifled a giggle. "Somehow, I don't think we're going to get any praise for that."

"Natalie!" Brian called, as if on cue. "Why don't

you help me gather up the equipment?"

"Um, sure," Natalie said, slightly taken aback. She headed toward the far end of the field and wrapped her arm around the goal net, dragging it toward the sports shed.

Once she got to the shed, Brian propped the door open for her. "Thanks, Nat, I really appreciate it," he said as she shoved the net through the doorway.

Natalie dusted her hands off on her shorts. "No problem." It was the least she could do, really, given that she had barely moved a muscle all through the sports period.

"So, I noticed that you're not exactly crazy about soccer," Brian observed.

Natalie looked up at him, the very picture of innocence. "Whatever gave you that idea?" she asked, wide-eyed. She could tell he knew she was being sarcastic.

"Wild guess." He ran his fingers through his curly red hair.

Brian looked so frustrated that Natalie actually felt a little guilty. "It's not you, Brian. I'm just, um, not really athletic. But, you know, I think you always find fun things for us to do in sports."

"Thanks, Natalie, but you don't need to reassure me. It's important to me that everyone here has a good time. You don't have to love every single thing we play, but if there's something you'd like to try, let me know. I mean, camp is—"

"—the time for new experiences, I know," Natalie said, cutting him off.

He grinned at her. "It's true."

"It must be, 'cause I keep hearing it," Natalie said, half-kidding. "Look, I'll think about it. I'm sure somehow, somewhere, there's some sort of sport that I like."

"Thanks, Natalie," Brian said.

"I could always be in charge of the whistle," Natalie offered, giggling.

"It's a thought," Brian agreed.

"I'd better go," Natalie said. "Lunch next. Can't miss it."

She ran to catch up to Alyssa, who looked at her quizzically. "Deep conversation?" Alyssa asked.

"He wants me to take a more active interest in sports," Natalie said. "Little does he know the most exercise I get at home is channel surfing." This was an exaggeration, but she was making a point.

"Yeah, it shows."

Natalie whirled around to find Chelsea slithering by. She looked perfect and rosy-cheeked, like an ad for a fitness club or a protein drink or something. *At least I'm not drenched in sweat,* Natalie thought to herself, *on the way to the mess hall.*

She didn't bother to say anything out loud, though. Chelsea just wasn't worth it.

SEVEN

Dear Hannah,

Greetings again from Camp Lake-puke.

I'm just kidding, really. It's not that bad. I mean, I still don't think I'm going to win Camper of the Year or anything, but for the most part I'm enjoying myself. Can you believe it's been almost a week?

Most of the girls here are cool. I really like this one chick, Alyssa, who is from South Jersey. She's very quiet and artsy—always writing or drawing in her journal. Anyway, her parents sent her to camp so she could learn to be more outgoing, but I think she's just fine the way she is. I mean, maybe she doesn't talk that much, but when she does, she always has something smart and funny to say. We're on the newspaper together—she's a really good writer. I guess you could say she's my best friend here. You would really like her.

The rest of the bunk is okay, too. Valerie is cool to hang out with—we're in nature together. Grace is the comedienne, always cracking jokes and making everyone laugh. She's really friendly and never wants anyone to be left out. Then there's Jenna, who has like a million brothers and sisters or at least three that I know of. Her twin, Adam, is very friendly and her older sister Stephanie is good friends with my CIT Marissa. And then I think there's one that's

off doing a college prep course. Or
something. I can't keep track. They've all
been coming to camp for, I think, a hundred
years or so, so she knows all the ropes. She's
kind of a tomboy and likes to play practical
jokes—which sometimes aren't so funny! It
doesn't bother me, but one of these days I
think she's really going to get into trouble.
And Alex is the big uber-camper who
knows all the counselors and never complains
and kicks total butt in every sport. It's a
little intimidating, even for me. She hangs
out with Sarah, who also loves sports, and
also this girl Brynn, who means well, but ...
well, she's a drama queen. Like last week,
during chores, she got stuck with the showers.
Mind you, the showers are gross, but we all
have to do it sooner or later—even me! The
way she carried on, you would have thought

she was the bunk slave or something. It's kind of annoying.

Still, the only girl I really have an issue with is Chelsea. She's really pretty—blond and skinny, you'd hate her—and also very athletic. But for some reason, she's got a total chip on her shoulder. I don't know what she's got against me—I mean, I'm obviously not vying for the Lakeview MVP award or anything. And it's not just me, either; she's always making little rude comments and not-jokes to people. I guess she's just got a bad attitude. Mostly, I try to ignore her and keep myself positive. Even NATURE'S not so bad these days.

Which brings me to Simon. Yes, the same guy I wrote you about that I met in the mess hall. Well, more like "bumped into," if you want the truth and all. But it turned

out he is also in nature, and after the first
session, he introduced himself to me (I had
to play cool and pretend like I hadn't
already gotten the whole 411 from Jenna,
since Adam is in his bunk!). It was kind of
awkward—I think he's a little shy. Not like
all those super-obnoxious boys from school!
He could tell I wasn't really "feeling" nature
and showed me little tricks, like how to feed
the rabbit and which leaves are poisonous
out in the wild. Personally, I'm planning to
avoid the wild at all costs, but Simon
doesn't have to know that! So that's an
interesting development, anyway. And it
kind of takes my mind off the fact that I
still haven't heard from Kyle Taylor yet (in
case you were wondering)! Too bad you're
not still in the city to spy for me!

Thanks for all your postcards—I save

them and tape them to the wall over my bed, right next to the picture of all of us skating in Central Park last winter. That way, I see your smiling face when the bugle (yes, a bugle—no joke) sounds at the crack of dawn. I think the Mona Lisa is my favorite. What a bummer that it was so crowded when you went! I haven't heard anything from Ellen or Kate, but Maggie wrote to tell me that her summer dance intensive is going well. Lucky girl—she gets to sleep in and spend the day working at the one thing she loves more than anything else! Meanwhile, I toil away at things like kickball and diving practice. Sigh...

I promise I'll write as soon as I've got anything new to report. Maybe I'll help Jenna pull the ultimate prank, and we'll both get kicked out. (KIDDING! Sort of.)

Or maybe I will free all the animals in the nature shack, and then Simon and I will gallop off into the sunset.

Whatever. I MISS YOU!!! You must be in Italy by now? Eat some pasta for me.

xoxo,
Nat

"Oh, that is so gross," Natalie said, shuddering.

"Come on, Nat—he likes you," Valerie said, sidling up to Natalie teasingly.

Natalie took a gi-normous step backward. "Seriously, stay away from me with that thing," she warned. "I can't believe you're even willing to touch it."

Valerie laughed, and patted the head of the snake that was now wound around her forearm. Valerie had made friends with all the animals in the nature shack, but she liked the snakes the best, and she always made fun of Natalie for being afraid of them.

"Just you wait until one bites you," Natalie warned.

"Afraid of a garter snake, Natalie?" Chelsea said incredulously. She always managed to make everything she said sound like an insult, Natalie noticed.

"I'm not scared," Natalie said hotly. "I just don't see a need to get up close and personal with something cold and slimy."

"For a city girl, you sure can be a baby," Chelsea said, and wandered off to play with the rabbits.

As soon as Chelsea was out of earshot, Natalie rolled her eyes at Valerie. "Funny, I've never seen *her* touch the snake," she commented. "She just likes to annoy me."

"She likes to annoy *everyone*," Valerie pointed out.

"But me especially," Natalie insisted.

Valerie shrugged. "Yeah, maybe. I wouldn't worry about it. She's probably just jealous."

"Of me? Why?" Natalie asked. "What'd I ever do to her?"

"Well, let's see, you're the only other girl in the bunk who's anywhere near as pretty as she is, and you also wear makeup and are into boys, just like her. So you're like some kind of big threat to her."

"That's ridiculous," Natalie scoffed. "She's the one who's totally gorgeous and always put-together. I think her body is naturally programmed to wake up before the bugle! And she's way more into camp than I am. I mean, she's good at all the sports and stuff. I'm no good at anything other than ballet and yoga. I'm, like, the anti-camper."

"It's not ridiculous, Natalie," Valerie protested. "For starters, you're an amazing swimmer, even if you hate to go in the lake. And let's not forget the one thing you've got that she *really* wants."

Natalie eyed her friend questioningly. Val winked and tilted her head in the direction of the rabbits, where

Chelsea was replenishing the animals' water. There was only one other person over by the rabbits. Simon.

"For starters, I do not 'have' Simon, and secondly— do you really think Chelsea likes him?" Natalie asked. But before Val could answer, Roseanne clapped her hands and called for everyone's attention.

"Girls, guys, gather round! I have an announcement to make," she said loudly.

But Natalie couldn't concentrate on what Roseanne was saying. She was still thinking about what Valerie had said. Simon did always go out of his way to talk with her in nature, which was nice, but she didn't know if he *liked* her, liked her. Or if she even wanted him to. Still, when she thought that maybe Chelsea was into Simon—well, the idea didn't make her feel very good. Not good at all.

But there were worse things to worry about at Camp Lakeview, as Natalie was about to learn.

"Next week, on Thursday, we're going on a camp-out," Roseanne said.

Suddenly, Chelsea's feelings for Simon were the least of Natalie's concerns.

▲ ▲ ▲

"What color today, Nat?" Marissa asked, spreading out a beach towel on the sand next to Natalie.

Natalie was a fantastic swimmer—she'd had all sorts of private lessons in New York. She didn't mind instructional swim, but she wasn't crazy about the lake and all of the actual fish that swam in it. So when free swim rolled around, she preferred to work on her tan.

The head of the waterfront, an extremely tan and fit counselor named Beth, seemed to think this was okay, though she was often trying new and inventive tactics at getting Natalie up and into the water. Just yesterday, she had tried to convince Natalie that lake water was good for the skin. While Natalie appreciated the approach— "A for effort, Beth," she'd said—she wasn't biting.

Natalie's new hobby was lying on the shore by the lake, painting her toes, and watching her bunkmates swim. Fortunately, free swim was the one thing in camp she could get out of if she wanted to, as long as she came down to the waterfront. Lately, Marissa had been joining her, which was especially cool because she always brought her magazines with her.

"Ice Princess," Natalie read off the bottom of the bottle. "Want me to do yours?" Her heart wasn't in it, though, after Roseanne's alarming announcement. Marissa instantly picked up on Natalie's mood.

"No, thanks, Steph did them for me after kitchen duty," Marissa said, wiggling her toes at Natalie by way of demonstration. "Passion Fruit."

"Nice," Natalie said approvingly.

"I brought *People* and *YM*, and if you're nice to me, I'll braid your hair," Marissa promised. "Steph's abandoning us today to flirt with Tyler." She indicated the swim shack, where, in fact, Jenna's older sister was attempting to read the palm of an older and *very* cute swim staffer. "She is shameless," Marissa commented. Then, sensing Natalie's mood, she asked, "What's wrong?"

"Did you know that I have to go on a camping trip with the nature group?" Natalie blurted out.

Marissa nodded her head. "Well, yeah. All the

specialties have something big they do sometime during the session. The drama kids do a play, the newspaper prints an issue, ceramics, arts and crafts, woodworking, and photography all have a 'gallery day' where they show their work. Didn't you know that?"

"I do now," Natalie said.

"I thought you were starting to like nature," Marissa pointed out.

"Hey, just because I've managed to avoid walking head-on into a poison-oak patch does not mean that I'm a born-again nature girl," Natalie said. "This trip sounds like bad news. We have to canoe out to some deserted island. When has anything good ever happened on a deserted island?" Natalie demanded.

Marissa laughed. "Slow down, drama queen," she said. "The nature kids go on the same trip every year, and nothing has ever gone wrong. I'm sure this year won't be any different."

Natalie glared at Marissa. "Okay, and then after we dock our boats, we have to hike—which I think is just a fancy term for walk, except maybe it's hilly and rocky and hard. Hike up a mountain, and then set up camp. And then we *cook* on the mountain and sleep there!"

"It's called 'roughing it,' " Marissa said. "Some people enjoy it."

"Not *this* people," Natalie said, frustrated. "I'm here, aren't I? I've tried to be a good sport. I eat the food. I sweep the porch. I come down to the lake during free swim. I haven't had access to my cell phone or e-mail since we got here. Marissa—" Natalie murmured, her voice lowering, "I even clean the toilets. I've *been* roughing it!"

"Well, do you want me to talk to Julie about getting you out of the trip?" Marissa asked with sincerity.

Natalie thought seriously for a moment. Did she? The idea was awfully appealing. It was easy to spot poison ivy in the clearing behind the nature shack, but she had a feeling the wilds on the deserted island would be more . . . well . . . *wild*. Nothing about the trip sounded like fun.

But.

She had promised Julie she would be strong, and for the most part, she had been. She had gotten to know Val, and liked her. She put up with Chelsea's snotty comments. She even learned a little something about nature. Just last week, Roseanne had complimented her on the bird-feeder that she'd built. So being strong wasn't so bad, and even though Natalie really didn't love nature, she wasn't a quitter. And besides, Simon would be on her trip.

Of course, so would Chelsea.

Simon. Think Simon, she reminded herself. That was a reason to go on the trip.

In fact, it might be all the reason she needed.

She turned to Marissa, squaring her shoulders with determination. "No," she said. "Don't worry about it. I'll go."

Marissa squealed and hugged her. "You rock! Scoot over then, sister. I'll braid your hair."

▲ ▲ ▲

Just before dinner that evening, Natalie and the rest of her bunkmates gathered outside the mess hall.

Before and after meals was a time when campers could really visit with friends from other bunks, or even other divisions, since everyone ate at the same time. Lots of campers chose to hang out on the steps of the mess hall itself, but Natalie still had the camping trip on her mind, and so she wasn't that interested in socializing. She wandered off a little ways down the path to a nearby wooden pagoda. Once she reached it, however, she realized it wasn't empty.

"Oh, I'm sorry," she said, retreating from the pagoda before she could intrude.

"No, hey, it's totally cool."

Natalie peered more closely into the pagoda and realized with a start that she had actually walked in on Simon! She flushed.

"I guess they haven't let us into the mess hall yet?" he asked.

Natalie shook her head no. "Not that I mind, to be honest."

Simon grinned. "True. I can't decide if it's a good thing or a bad thing that I'm a vegetarian. On the plus side, I get to avoid the random mystery meats. On the other hand, the selection leaves a *lot* to be desired."

"You're a vegetarian?" Natalie asked, nearly swooning. To her, that sounded very cosmopolitan. Almost New York, even.

"Yeah, why? Are you?"

Natalie nodded. "Yeah. I mean no. I mean, I was," she finished, appalled at her awkwardness.

"Why'd you give it up?" Simon asked, sounding genuinely curious.

"Well, I don't eat too much meat, but I guess I just

decided that I couldn't go without sushi. It was just too much of a sacrifice. Plus, half the time, it's all that my mom and I even eat," she explained.

Simon raised an eyebrow. "Sushi? Wow. Raw fish—that's pretty brave."

Natalie giggled. "Brave? Hardly. You're talking to the girl who lives in terror of poison oak. I'm like, totally freaked about our camping trip," she confessed.

"It's nothing," Simon assured her. "It can even be fun, I promise."

"I'll believe that when I see it," Natalie said.

"I swear," Simon insisted. "Roseanne does this trip every year, and she hasn't lost a camper yet. I did it last year."

"So you're like a seasoned pro," Natalie teased.

"Totally," Simon said. "I can be your guide."

Yes, yes, you can, Natalie thought to herself. She racked her brain to come up with a reply that wouldn't sound lame or over-eager but came up empty. *Say something, Nat,* she begged herself.

"Nat!"

Natalie looked up to see who was calling her.

"Dinner! Come on! We're all going in!"

It was Jenna. Normally, Jenna's loud voice, bright eyes, and bouncing ponytail were a source of amusement for Natalie, but right now Nat could have killed the girl for her timing.

"Oh, ah," she hemmed, not wanting to walk away from the conversation with Simon.

Simon stood up and dusted himself off. "You go," he said to Natalie. "We'll have plenty of time to talk on the hike, right?" He winked at her and walked off to rejoin his own bunk.

"Ooooh, Natalie, do you have a *boyfriend?*" Jenna singsonged.

Natalie whirled around as if just then realizing that Jenna was still there. She was completely unfazed by Jenna's little joke. "We'll see," she said, with a little smile on her face. "We'll see."

At dinner, everyone in 3C was talking about all the activities they had planned in their specialties. "Will you read my newspaper piece before it's published?" Alyssa asked Natalie shyly. The girls had learned that professional writers called their articles "pieces," and they liked to use the grown-up terminology.

Natalie pushed a rubbery piece of chicken back and forth across her plate. Maybe it was time to reconsider vegetarianism again? At least for the summer, anyhow. "Of course. I mean, if you'll read mine," she said. She had conducted an interview with Brian, the sports counselor, on what had prompted him to come over from Australia for the summer, and she was really excited about it, but she knew that Alyssa was the better writer. Alyssa would definitely give her piece a great once-over. "I *may* have gone on a little too long about his accent," Natalie joked.

"How could you not? It's so cool!" Alyssa agreed.

"The best part is that he let me give the interview *instead* of taking sports!" Nat exclaimed, causing Alyssa to nearly choke on her food in laughter.

"Ow," Alyssa grimaced as Jenna slid into the

bench next to her, giggling mischievously. "And you're sitting on my lap because . . ."

"Sorry," Jenna said, slightly breathless. She was peering across the table, over Alex's shoulder, to the table behind them.

"What did you do?" Alex asked, her eyes narrowing suspiciously. Of all the girls in 3C, Alex was most disapproving of Jenna's pranks, mainly because she hated to get into trouble herself.

"Nothing," Jenna said, but she looked ready to burst out of her seat with excitement.

"Something," Sarah, who sat directly to Alex's right, chimed in softly. "Definitely something."

Suddenly, the boys at the table jumped up, all mumbling variations on "ugh," "ew," and "gross." Jenna burst out laughing.

"Isn't that your brother's bunk's table?" Sarah asked Jenna.

But Jenna just looked off to her right, humming a little bit to herself. Whatever she'd done to her brother and his bunkmates, she wasn't telling. And it looked like for now, at least, she wasn't going to be found out.

Natalie knew that whatever joke Jenna had pulled, it was probably really funny. Just like last week, when she had hidden all the silverware from 3A's lunch table. But she was worried about her friend. That was just Natalie's way, when she cared about someone. What if Jenna's little practical schemes were actually a sign of a bigger problem, like something that was on Jenna's mind? Or, if they weren't a sign of a problem, they were going to be the cause of one, soon. How long could she get away with these pranks before she got into serious trouble?

chapter
EIGHT

"So, making s'mores is actually really easy—" Jenna explained. She held out a graham cracker and a square of milk chocolate in preparation for a big demonstration.

"—believe it or not, J, I've actually had s'mores before," Natalie said, cutting Jenna off before she could launch into the full-blown lecture. She really liked Jenna, but the girl had at some point decided to "adopt" Natalie and show her the ins and outs of camp. Which was great in theory, but Natalie was independent by nature, and not too crazy about being adopted. Still, she tried to be patient. She knew Jenna was just being nice.

"I thought you'd never been to camp before. When did you make s'mores?" Alex asked, overhearing the girls' conversation.

"Oh, there's a restaurant in New York that will bring them right to your table for you. You cook the marshmallows on these little burners. It's so cool," Natalie said, feeling a little wave of homesickness pass through her. What surprised her, though, was that it was just that—a *little* wave of homesickness. Could it be that she was actually starting to *enjoy* herself at camp? Too weird.

"Maybe you're just too *sophisticated* for sleepaway camp," Chelsea said. She didn't make it sound like a compliment.

"Yes, well, I left my diamonds back in the city. I figured I can do without them for the summer, dahling," Natalie laughed, putting on a fake "proper" accent. She had decided that the best thing to do with Chelsea was to pretend that her comments were intended as light-hearted jokes—even when they obviously weren't. So far, the tactic seemed to be working. Chelsea pursed her lips but she didn't say another word.

From across the campfire, Alyssa nodded to Natalie—a tiny, almost imperceptible gesture. Someone else might not have even noticed it, but Nat knew that her friend was giving her props for not letting Chelsea get to her.

It was Tuesday night, and bunk 3C was having a cookout. After all the camp food, Natalie could understand why so many campers got so excited over barbecued hot dogs and hamburgers. She had eaten one of each, herself, and even though she was stuffed, she still managed to find a tiny bit of room leftover for s'mores. She hated to admit it, but there was something cool about roasting marshmallows over an open camp-fire—not more special than having them brought to your table in a New York City restaurant, but different. Good different.

The girls in her bunk were good different, too, Natalie had decided. Even though she still wasn't thrilled with things like spiders in the bathrooms and bug juice for lunch, the girls in 3C had a nice chemistry. Even now, they were all huddled in one large circle, stuffing themselves with graham crackers, chocolate, and marshmallows. Julie and Marissa were off to one side of the barbecue talking to Pete, who had manned the grill, and a few of his kitchen buddies, including one named LJ who Natalie really liked. LJ was really funny. He refused to tell her what his initials stood for. He told all the girls in 3C that if they were lucky, he'd let them know at the closing banquet, at the end of the summer.

"Have you girls had your fill?" Kathleen, the head of the third division, walked by, smiling knowingly. Kathleen was energetic and always friendly, and could tell by the girls' expressions that they had eaten more than enough for the evening.

"Oh, gosh, I'll never eat again," Grace moaned, dropping the long stick with her marshmallow to the ground beside her. She bent over and clutched her stomach dramatically.

Kathleen grinned again. "I sort of doubt that," she said, and wandered over to speak with Julie and Marissa.

"Alex, you were smart not to have any," Grace said, still feigning her stomachache. "I really need to learn some limits."

"Oh, well, uh, you know—I like to take care of myself, for soccer, you know," Alex replied. Natalie looked up. Was it her imagination, or did Alex look slightly uncomfortable? But what would she have to feel uncomfortable about? So she didn't eat junk food. So what?

Natalie offered up her best fake burp. All the girls shrieked with laughter.

"Ugh, that is *so* gross," Brynn said, giggling. "Does *Simon* think that's cute?"

Natalie blushed. "What are you talking about?"

Brynn rolled her eyes. "Oh, come on, it's so obvious. You completely stare at him every time we're in the mess hall. You luuuuuv him," she sang.

"Okay, fine, he's cute, so what?" Natalie protested.

Grace made little gagging noises. "Cute, yak. Boys are icky, not cute."

"Oh, come on," Natalie insisted. "You're telling me there's not a single boy in camp you'd be into?"

All the girls shook their heads emphatically. "It must be something in the Manhattan water, Nat," Sarah said. "You're the only one so far."

"You make it sound like I have some kind of disease," Natalie said, laughing. "Whatever. At least this way I don't have to worry about any of you guys going after him!" She glanced at Chelsea as she said this. But Chelsea was focused intently on fishing out a graham cracker from a newly opened box and didn't—or wouldn't—look up.

"My dad says I can't go on a date until I'm in high school," Karen said. "That's fine by me. Anyway, we play board games on Friday nights. He's a teacher, and sometimes he makes up cool games all on his own."

"Oh, that's so fun!" Candace said. "My dad's a boring lawyer and the only thing he brings home is his laptop."

"Mine's a lawyer, too," Alex put in. "It looks like the dullest job in the world. Whenever we go on vacation, he spends half the time screaming into his cell phone." She shifted her weight and stretched her legs out in front of her, closer to the warmth of the fire. "What about you, Natalie? You never talk about your father," she said.

"Huh?" Natalie said, stalling for time. "He's, uh . . . well, my parents are divorced."

"Oh, that's hard," Sarah said sympathetically. "Do you see him often?"

Natalie shrugged. "Sometimes," she said. "He lives out west. What about yours?" she asked, trying to push the spotlight off herself.

"He's an orthodontist," Sarah replied. "So my older sister got her braces for cheap!"

"Hey, Natalie, when's your campout?" Jenna asked suddenly, a twinkle appearing in her eye.

"Thursday night," Natalie answered, suddenly suspicious. "Why?"

"Well, speaking of boys, I have a fun idea of how we can pass the time between now and then."

"What, you mean instead of evening activity?" Natalie asked. She wouldn't have minded getting out of evening activity. But for some reason, she didn't think that was quite what Jenna was getting at.

"Oh, no—I meant for after," Jenna said quickly. "Later—*much* later—I've got plans for us. *All* of us," she added dramatically.

Natalie glanced around the campfire nervously. She wasn't so sure she liked the sound of that.

▲ ▲ ▲

That evening after the cookout, the girls were all excitable as they prepared for bed. Even Julie could see that something was up.

"Ladies, you're all so hyper tonight. I hope you don't have some sort of mischief planned," she said.

Natalie sort of hoped so, too. But then, a part of her thought that whatever Jenna had in mind could really be fun. So basically, she wasn't sure what to think.

After the girls had all gotten into their bunks, Marissa read to them from the "Trauma-rama" section of *YM*. This was their favorite thing to do before lights-out. Usually, the stories were completely outrageous, and Marissa made the girls vote which ones they thought were true, and which were made-up.

"MADE-UP!" Alex shouted from her bed after an especially colorful entry. "Please. Who ever really sneezes that much snot?"

"Point taken," Marissa said, closing the magazine.

"Okay, girls, Marissa and I have to go out for a little bit," Julie said. This wasn't a surprise. Julie and Marissa usually went outside for a while after lights-out. No one was totally sure what they did. The counselors rotated their evenings off, and those that had off definitely left camp. Natalie couldn't blame them. There were always two counselors per division—one guy and one girl—who were "OD," or "on-duty," as well, and it was their job to patrol at night and make sure that things were okay with all the campers in their division. But those who weren't off or OD managed to disappear just the same. Jenna's theory was that all the counselors met at the big rock where afternoon snack was held, not too far away from the bunks. "We have a meeting with the rest of the staff. Mark and Kerri are OD tonight. Do you promise you'll all behave?"

"Yes, Julie," the girls chorused in a mocking singsong.

After the door had swung shut behind them, the bunk was quiet for a moment. No one wanted to be the first to speak what was on everyone's mind.

Finally, Jenna sat up in bed. "Do you think they're gone?"

Alex got out of her bed and walked over to the front door. She opened it and peered out. "The coast is clear. No Mark, no Kerri, no problem." She padded back to her bed and sat on the edge of it. "So what were you thinking?"

The lights were still out, but Natalie could practically feel a sly grin creep its way across Jenna's face. "Raid," she whispered.

"Awesome!" Alex said. Even though Alex hated to get in trouble, she was willing to risk it for something like a raid, because raids were just too much fun to resist. She slid back off her bed and poked around in her cubby, pulled out her flashlight, and flicked it on.

"Careful with that thing," Chelsea said, squinting from the bright light. "What is a raid, anyway?"

Natalie was glad Chelsea had asked, since she herself had no idea.

Alex squealed and settled back down on the edge of her bed. "Oooh, it's SO much fun. We sneak out and into someone's bunk—"

"—a *boys'* bunk—" Jenna cut in.

"—yeah, yeah, boys' bunk," Alex continued, looking slightly annoyed at being interrupted. "And, you know, we tp—toilet paper—their bunk and do all sorts of other things while they're sleeping. Like we can put toothpaste on their toilet seats or hide all their toilet paper—"

"So basically we're sabotaging their bathroom?" Natalie asked.

Alex shot her a look. "Well, not necessarily. But that's the kind of thing that's going to get to them."

"*I* always like to tape their bathroom doors shut and pull all their covers down while they're sleeping," Jenna said. There was an edge to her voice that suggested that she didn't really like being upstaged by Alex.

"Do you ever get caught?" Karen asked softly.

"Nah," Jenna bragged. "I mean, it's harmless."

"Counselors practically *expect* you to do it," Alex agreed. "So if you keep it safe and stuff, no one ever says anything."

Natalie found herself warming to the idea. But she still had one question. "Um, which bunk are we going to raid?" she asked.

Jenna snorted. "Every year, I like to raid Adam's bunk," she said. "So, 3F. Is that okay with you, *Nat*?" she finished meaningfully.

Simon's bunk, Natalie thought. *Of course.* "Yeah, sure," she said, trying to act casual.

"I had a feeling it would be," Jenna teased. "Okay, who else is in?"

It turned out that almost everyone was game. Karen was nervous, but she put aside her fears after Alex and Jenna both reassured her that they wouldn't get in any trouble. Candace said she'd rather stay back and read, but she gave in when Sarah guilted her about "acting as a bunk." And that was really it. Chelsea, in particular, seemed very excited. As soon as Jenna had explained her plan, she had hopped out of bed to change into her cutest drawstring capris. Natalie guessed it probably didn't matter what they wore.

But she put on a clean pair of jeans, just in case.

"Well, I guess you were wrong about where the counselors go at night," Alex said to Jenna. The bunk was maneuvering slowly, ducking behind bushes when possible, and they were just rounding the big, central rock. They had tiptoed out the front door of the bunk un-detected easily enough—the OD counselors were clearly otherwise occupied. The rock was completely unpopulated. Alex sounded fairly pleased about it. To Natalie, it seemed like Alex and Jenna were locked in a bizarre competition to be the one who knew the most about camp. *Silly*, she thought. *So not worth it.*

Suddenly, someone stomped on her foot. She almost cried out, but the offender clapped a hand over her mouth, muffling the sound. She turned to find Alyssa smiling at her. "Sorry!" she whispered. "I tripped."

"That's what you get for wearing flip-flops," Natalie said. She had tried to convince her friend to wear trail shoes, but Alyssa wasn't having it. "My feet need to breathe," she had protested.

"You win," Alyssa admitted.

"Then why am I the one with the squashed toe, Ms. Breathy-foot?" Natalie kidded.

"Girls!" Alex said in the loudest whisper she could manage. "We're almost there. Keep it down!"

"She is so out of control," Alyssa mumbled.

Natalie almost broke into a giggle, but Alyssa reached out and covered her mouth again.

"Good thing we know how to identify poison oak, right?" Valerie said, catching up to Natalie and Alyssa. "And you thought nature was pointless."

"Not like I could even see it if I were standing right in a poison-oak patch! It's pitch-black out here!" Natalie pointed out.

"Girls!" Jenna said, sounding like Julie. "We're going in. Now, you all have your assignments. Alyssa and Nat, you're going in first. You're going to take the toilet paper out of the bathroom. Then you'll pass it off to Grace and Valerie, who will tp the bunk beds. Meanwhile, Sarah and Brynn will put shaving cream on the toilet seats. Jessie, Alex, and Candace are in charge of rounding up the garbage cans and lining them up outside the front door. That way, they'll topple when the boys try to leave in the morning. Chelsea and Karen are going to hide the shower curtains."

"What will you do?" Natalie asked.

"Oh, I've got special plans of my own for Adam," Jenna said mysteriously.

"Poor Adam," Grace said, sympathetically.

"How about a huddle before we go in?" Alex suggested.

Jenna glared at Alex, but the girls were already grouping together. In the dark, they leaned in to one another and placed all of their hands on top of one another's in the center of the huddle. "Go, 3C!" they whisper-shouted.

Natalie crept up to the front door with Alyssa at her heels. "This may be a dumb idea," Natalie mumbled, suddenly having second thoughts. "But here goes nothing," she said quietly, and pulled the door open.

Instantly, all the girls were engulfed. Natalie was pelted squarely in the stomach with a stream of water, while at the same time covered from head to toe in shaving cream.

"Oh, what the—" Natalie shouted, only to be rewarded by a blast of water into her mouth. She sputtered to herself as the sounds of male war cries filled the room.

Before Natalie could make sense of the scene, her bunkmates had rushed in, screeching with their own war whoops. Jenna whipped a mini water pistol from the waistband of her capri pants and fired from the hip. Karen freaked out, bolted for the bathroom, and locked herself in a stall. Chelsea ran up and down the bunk weaving toilet paper from bed to bed.

Jenna, though, stood stock-still, assessing the scene. Finally, she put her fingers to her lips and whistled.

The bunk was silent.

"*Adam,*" she said, her voice dangerously low.

From the far corner of the bunk, the girls heard chuckling. "Gotcha, sis!" A head full of light brown curls emerged, followed by a male-looking version of Jenna in hospital scrubs and a concert T-shirt.

"How did you know?" Jenna demanded.

"Give me a break, Jenna. I'm on to you. I'm *always* on to you," he said. "I mean, did you think I didn't know what you did with the bug juice the other day?" he continued.

Jenna pursed her lips, planted her hands on her

hips, and waited for him to go on.

"And by the way, you plan a raid just about this time *every* summer, J. So this wasn't exactly the hugest shock."

"Well, how did you know it would be tonight?" Jenna asked.

"It makes perfect sense. The counselors are all at that big meeting."

"What big meeting?" Natalie interrupted, suddenly worried. "Julie said they were meeting the other counselors. You know, at the rock. You said they always go to the rock!" she said, turning to face Jenna. But then she remembered. *When we walked past the rock, there was no one around.*

Adam nodded. "Most nights, they do. And you would never have been able to get past them."

"Hey!" Alex protested.

Adam ignored her. "But tonight, they had a meeting with Dr. Steve."

"Dr. Steve? As in, director of the camp Dr. Steve?" Sarah asked, a tinge of dread creeping into her voice.

Natalie understood why she sounded that way. Dr. Steve was very friendly—he made it a point to visit all the activities during the day, and to talk to all the campers—but he was not a pushover. And she didn't think he'd be the kind to look the other way if he found out some campers had gone on a raid while their counselors were out.

"Well, no big deal, right?" came a voice from the corner.

Natalie whirled around to see Simon standing near the front door. He was wearing cut-off sweat pants and a T-shirt with Bart Simpson across the front. *He likes The Simpsons? I like The Simpsons,* Natalie thought. *We're perfect for each other!* She realized she was spacing and forced herself to concentrate on what he was saying.

"All they have to do is get back before the meeting's over, and Dr. Steve will never know," he pointed out.

"Right," Natalie said. "That makes sense. But it means we have to get going, like, now. If the counselors come back, that means the meeting's over."

"Duh," Chelsea chimed in. Natalie instantly felt stupid for suggesting something so obvious.

"Well, she's right," Simon countered.

Natalie couldn't believe it. Was Simon *defending* her? "Are you guys okay to clean up by yourselves?" she asked. She felt bad just leaving with everything such a mess.

Adam laughed. "No worries. It's too bad, though—usually raids turn into parties. We would have shared some of our junk-food stash with you."

"Next time," Natalie said, smiling.

"Uh, you guys, there may be a little problem with the plan," Alex said, breaking into the moment.

"Such as?" Jenna asked nervously.

"Such as, where's Alyssa? Nat, wasn't she supposed to come in first with you?"

Natalie glanced around the bunk nervously. Where *was* Alyssa, anyway? "Oh, no," she groaned. "I told her not to wear flip-flops! What if she slipped outside or something?"

In a flash, Natalie and Alex dashed outside, where they immediately found Alyssa kneeled on the porch and clutching her shin.

"I'm the biggest klutz in the world," Alyssa said sheepishly. "Look." She extended her leg. "I *really* shouldn't have worn flip-flops, Nat."

Natalie gasped. "I won't even say 'I told you so,'" she promised. Alyssa had mangled her leg really badly. It was raw and oozing, and the ankle was looking a little bit puffy, as well. Alex and Natalie quickly helped her back into the bunk so that the group could assess the situation together.

"Oh, jeez. We need to take you to the infirmary and get that cleaned out," Natalie said. "What if you sprained your ankle?"

"The infirmary's closed," Grace said. "Plan B?"

Natalie's stomach turned over. "Uh, I think the only real plan B is to go find the counselors." The thought was not appealing.

Jenna's face went white. "We can't! Julie will *kill* me!"

"Jenna, look at her leg!" Natalie pressed. "What would you rather we do?"

"I have some Band-Aids in the bunk," Jenna offered.

"Jen, I'm sorry, but look at that. It's, like, dripping, and not even ankle-shaped. I don't think your Band-Aids are going to do the trick. Can you even walk on that, Alyssa?"

Alyssa leaned into her leg tentatively. "It's sore," she admitted.

Simon stepped forward. "Why don't you let Nat and me walk you to find the counselors?" he suggested. "I mean, it was her idea, but you know, if you can't walk or whatever, I could carry you better than she could."

Natalie didn't know if Alyssa really needed two personal escorts, but she wasn't about to argue. Besides, how sweet was it of Simon to offer? "Sounds like a plan," she said, crossing over to where Alyssa stood.

"That's ridiculous," Chelsea cut in. "Simon, I can go with you."

Natalie seethed. How low could Chelsea stoop?

"It's okay, Chelsea. It looks like Nat's got this covered," Simon insisted.

It was all Natalie could do not to stick out her tongue and do a little victory dance in Chelsea's face. *Be the bigger person,* she reminded herself.

"Whatever," Chelsea snapped.

Natalie decided to take charge. After all, Simon seemed to think that she knew what she was talking about. "Okay, um, Alyssa, why don't you put one arm across my shoulder and one arm across Simon's?"

Alyssa maneuvered forward and awkwardly draped one arm over each of them. The three of them hopped toward the front door like losers in a strange three-legged relay, when suddenly the door opened, and the overhead lights flew on. The room was blindingly bright.

"It's the mother ship!" Grace shrieked.

"Shh!" Natalie said. "*So* not the time for jokes."

"*What* is going on here?!"

It was Nate, the counselor for 3F. He didn't look very pleased.

And standing beside him was Julie.

chapter NINE

"I can't believe Julie let you off with just a warning!" Grace said, reaching over Natalie to grab the pitcher of milk that stood in the middle of the breakfast table.

"I know, she was really cool about it," Jenna agreed. "But she was *not* pleased. She made it clear that this was my last get-out-of-jail-free." She shook her head, causing her sandy ponytail to bob up and down. "I'm just relieved that Dr. Steve didn't find out. If he had, I don't think Julie would have been so understanding."

"What did you even tell Nurse Helen, anyway, Alyssa?" Grace asked.

In the end, Julie had gone with Natalie and Alyssa to the nurse. They had explained that Alyssa had been "outside" and had tripped, and Nurse Helen had been good enough to leave it at that. She took a look at Alyssa's ankle and declared it not sprained, cleaned it out, wrapped it in an Ace bandage, and sent the girls on their way. Today, Alyssa was still limping slightly, but was basically okay.

Just then, Simon walked to their table with a

group of his friends.

"Hey!" Natalie called out, getting Simon's attention. "Thanks for offering to help me take her. That was cool of you."

"Oh, no problem. But you were awesome," Simon said.

"Huh? What do you mean?" Natalie asked, surprised.

"Well, just the way that you took charge," Simon explained. "You knew that the only answer was to go to the infirmary, even if it meant getting in trouble, and you were willing to go and accept the consequences. Not everyone would have done that."

"Well, I mean, when your friend is practically an amputee," Natalie joked, shrugging off the compliment.

"Come on, Nat. You would have done that no matter who was hurt," Simon insisted. Natalie couldn't decide which was more exciting—hearing Simon say such nice things about her—or the fact that he was calling her "Nat." She liked hearing him use her nickname, like they were old friends.

"Excuse me, Simon," Chelsea cut in. "But I believe the boys' table is over there." She pointed to the other side of the mess hall.

Natalie rolled her eyes as Simon walked off.

"I'm sure he'll talk to you at the campout," Alyssa whispered.

"The campout? That's hardly going to be my finest hour!" Natalie groaned. She flung her head down onto the table in mock despair.

"You do realize you're getting cornflakes in your hair," Grace said dryly.

When breakfast was over, the girls slowly filed out of the mess hall. It was gray and overcast as the girls stepped outside.

"What do you think's going on over *there?*" Brynn asked suddenly, stopping short.

Natalie glanced over to where Brynn was pointing, just a few paces in front of the mess hall. Sure enough, an enormous stretch limo idled on the dirt path, and in front of it stood a small entourage of rock-star types—a super-skinny blonde; a tall, beefy man in black; and a small, nervous, wiry type. From where she stood, Natalie couldn't quite make out who the would-be celebrities were, especially since they were completely mobbed by campers. But she had some idea.

"Oh my God!" she heard one girl from an older division yell. "I LOVE you!"

"Dude, your last movie *rocked!*"

"Can I have your autograph?"

"What are you *doing* here?"

"Is that your limo, man? Sweet!"

Natalie's stomach lurched, and a feeling of dread washed over her.

"Oh my *God!*" Brynn shouted, recognition dawning. "I can't believe it!"

"That's Tad Maxwell!" Alex shrieked excitedly. "*What* is he doing here?" Her faced turned bright red. "I think I'm going to hyperventilate. I mean, I'm his biggest fan! I can't *believe* it! I just can't *believe* it!"

"Alex, relax. You're gonna blow a gasket," Natalie

said, uncomfortable.

Alex whirled around to Natalie, eyes flashing with excitement. "Of *course* I am, Nat! Do you even *realize* who that is? That's Tad Maxwell! *Spy in the Big City* Tad Maxwell. *Spy in the Far East* Tad Maxwell! *Spy in the Jungle* Tad Maxwell! And he's here! Right before our eyes! I mean, it's not a poster, it's really him! That's Tad Maxwell! That's—"

"—that's my father," Natalie finished.

Then she turned and ran away.

"I'm sorry."

Natalie tilted her head up to regard her father. He did look genuinely sorry to have surprised her.

"I thought it'd be fun for you," he insisted.

After her terrible experience at the mess hall, Natalie had run back to the bunk as fast as she possibly could. But once she was there, she didn't know what to do with herself. After all, her secret was out now. And it wasn't like anyone wouldn't find her back at the bunk. Not to mention, her father was here on one of his unexpected visits, and she had to face him sooner or later.

She really, really wished it could be later. But no such luck.

The thing was, Natalie really liked her father. He was fun and sweet, and she totally knew how much he loved her. Unfortunately, his work was very demanding, and he was often away on location for months at a time. When he wasn't on location, he was touring to promote his latest movie or shooting magazine covers or training for his next role . . . one way or another, he was always occupied. And so Natalie had learned to appreciate him when he was around, but not to expect more of him than he was able to give. It was sad, but it was life. The most important thing was that she had a mother and a father who both cared about her.

Back in New York, Natalie went to a pretty fancy private school. Most of her friends were either the children of celebrities, or else their parents were just so rich that they couldn't even be bothered with the whole starstruck thing. Hannah's mother, for example, was an African ambassador, and their friend Maggie's mother was actual royalty, though Natalie couldn't even pronounce the name of the country that she came from.

Natalie's friends thought the fact that her father was a big-time action hero was pretty cool. But it really wasn't a big deal to them. Natalie never knew how other people would react to the information. Some kids were really weirded out and just assumed she was a snob or spoiled or something. Others got really nicey-nice, wanting to get in and meet a real-life movie star. Natalie was tired of people seeing her for who her father was first, before they got to know her on her own terms.

So when her mother first told her about "Operation Lake-puke," Natalie had decided that she wasn't going to tell anyone about her father. For once, she wanted to be anonymous. It would be nice, she decided, to be just "Natalie"—no strings attached.

Fat chance of that now. For Pete's sake—he'd brought his girlfriend, his bodyguard, and his personal assistant! To *Lakeview*! Not exactly low-profile . . .

Natalie's father had eventually tracked her down

to her bunk. Julie had suggested that they go out on the porch to talk privately, which was where they now sat. Her father explained that he was between shoots and wanted to stop by and see how her summer was going. He seemed really sorry that he had just popped in like that.

Natalie sighed. "It's not your fault," she said. "I know you were trying to do something special."

"You used to like it when I surprised you," he pointed out.

"I did! I mean, I do. But I was really liking the way that no one knew who you were," she said. Her father looked hurt. "I mean—well, it was cool to be meeting people on my own terms, you know? I mean, I didn't want anyone to act weird or different once they knew who you were. I wanted them to like me for me. Or not like me for me, whatever. You get the point."

Her father smiled and pushed her hair back from her face. "Believe it or not, Nat, I know exactly what you mean. I have to deal with that every day. Agents, actors, directors—everyone telling me what I want to hear."

Natalie smirked at him. "That must be awful."

He laughed. "Well, okay, not always. Point taken."

"You look good," she said. "The 'spy' training is always a good thing." And he did look good. He was tanned and fit and actually even looked relaxed, which was rare for him.

Her father fake-flexed a bicep. "Not bad for an old-timer, right?" he laughed.

"One of the girls in my bunk has your poster up on the wall," Natalie said. "She thinks you're cute. It's pretty gross."

Her father arched an eyebrow. "Gross? Should I be offended?"

Natalie giggled. "Sorry." She stood up and walked toward him. "I'm glad to see you."

Her father reached out and pulled her close for a hug. "I'm glad to see you, too, sweetie."

She pushed away and looked at him again. "What have you got on tap for today? I'd give you the grand tour but even with all your personal training I don't think you could handle the *real* great outdoors," she teased. "Also, you wouldn't be able to walk a foot in any direction without being attacked by legions of fans."

"Well, hang on, that could be fun," her father protested, pretending to consider his options. "Legions, you say? ... Nah, I get enough of that in LA," he decided. "How about I bust you out of this joint for the afternoon? I already cleared it with Dr. Steve. Who, by the way, does not strike me as a medical professional. Has your mother checked his credentials? Anyway, we could do lunch, go shopping—"

"Shopping? Please don't be kidding," Natalie said, eyes lighting up at the prospect.

"Of course I'm not kidding! Josie couldn't go a day without spending some of my money."

Natalie knew that her father's girlfriend, Josie, *loved* to shop.

"I don't know what sort of shops we'll find up here," Natalie warned her father.

"Oh, I'm not worried. Somehow, between you and Josie, I bet we can sniff out the bargains," her father said, patting her on the head. "I have one call to make—"

"How very Hollywood of you—" Natalie quipped.

"—and then I'll get Skylar to bring the car up," her father finished, ignoring her.

"Don't be ridiculous, Dad. Go make your call, and I'll meet you at the front entrance to the camp. No more drama, okay?" Natalie said.

"Fine." He kissed her on her forehead. "See you in fifteen."

Her father trotted off in the direction of the camp entrance, and Natalie squared her shoulders and prepared herself to go back into the bunk. She had no idea what she was going to say to any of her friends, but it was now or never.

As she walked into the bunk, she was aware of the room going utterly silent. She suddenly had the distinct impression that just moments before, she'd been the subject of conversation. *Don't be paranoid, Nat,* she told herself, but she couldn't shake the sensation that all eyes were on her. She kept her head down as she crossed to her cubby to fish out her bag.

"How's your father, Nat?" Julie chirped, breaking the silence.

"Um, he's okay," Natalie managed. "Tired, I guess, because he just finished filming."

Julie didn't seem to know what else to say. In the end, she decided on a nondescript, "mmm," before turning back to her book.

"God, he is really great-looking in person."

Natalie turned to find Chelsea gazing at her with stars in her eyes. It was like she'd had some sort of personality transplant or something.

Just what I didn't want to happen, Natalie thought, dejected. She glanced up to Alyssa's bunk—but all she could see were feet. Alyssa was either sleeping or playing dead. Natalie hoped she was sleeping.

"Why didn't you say anything?" Alex said. She looked a little bit sad. "We wouldn't have cared. But I feel so stupid for all of those times I went on about him, and he—he was your father . . ." Her voice trailed off.

"I know," Natalie whispered. "I just . . ."

Just what? she asked herself. But she just couldn't come up with a good enough answer. "I'm sorry," she finished finally. "I have to go. I'll be back later."

"Sure!" Julie agreed. Her enthusiasm was out of sync with the mood of the room.

Natalie trudged out the front door, wondering how she was going to make things right with her friends. Why had she lied to them? Why had she hidden the truth about her family? How could she expect them to trust her again?

"Hey, uh, can I talk to you?"

Natalie looked up and gasped. "Simon," she said. "I, uh . . . what's up?" *Duh. What's up is that your father is a movie star and you never said anything and now everyone thinks you're weird and secretive and probably all stuck-up and spoiled. That's what's up.*

"So, uh . . . your father. Tad Maxwell," Simon said, stating the obvious.

"Yup," Natalie said, swinging her arms back and forth nervously. "That he is. And I, um, didn't want to say anything . . . I don't know why I didn't want to say anything," she said at last. "I guess I suck. I wouldn't blame you if you were mad at me." *Oh, please don't be mad at me,* Natalie thought.

"Well, it's just—"

Natalie's heart dropped to her stomach. "Well, it's just" was not the same thing as "of course I'm not mad." Not at all. And suddenly, she wasn't sure she wanted to hear the end of that sentence. Her friends were upset with her, her secret was out, and now Simon—well, whatever was on his mind, it was too much. She couldn't deal with it just then. And her father was still waiting for her down at the entrance to the camp.

"Look, I'm really sorry, okay?" she said pleadingly. "I know I wasn't completely honest with you. And I know you probably hate me. But I can't talk right now. My father . . . my father's waiting. And I have to meet him. Now." She turned and began to walk off down the path, doing her best to ignore the hurt look in Simon's eyes.

Quickly, almost against her own will, she turned back again. He was still staring at her, looking very confused and disappointed. "I'm sorry," she repeated.

Then she took off to find her father.

chapter TEN

"Well, Natalie, I do have to give you credit. I don't know if I would be able to survive in the wilderness all summer long," Josie said, delicately picking at a salad.

After several hours of attempting to shop, Natalie and Josie had finally given in and accepted that rural Pennsylvania didn't have that much to offer them. There were lots of cute crafts shops and antiquey places, but the truth was that Tad's house in LA was totally done out in an ultra-mod design, and none of the things they would find in Pennsylvania would really mesh with his decor. And the outlet shops, it turned out, were hours away. Once the trio had gotten past the disappointment (well, Natalie and Josie had been disappointed, and Tad had just done his best to seem sympathetic), they opted to drown their sorrows in milkshakes and burgers at the nearest roadside stop. Her father thought it would be great fun to eat at an authentic diner. Josie, however, was accustomed to healthy California food and was busily picking out the cheese and croutons from her salad.

Natalie laughed. "It's not quite the 'wilderness,'

you know. I think you just got the wrong impression when they told you they didn't have low-fat dressing here. I mean, we do have running water and indoor toilets." She flashed back to the spider she'd encountered on her first day of camp and shuddered. "Most of the time," she amended. "Anyway, I'm told it builds character."

Her father laughed heartily. "Kid, I think you've got more than enough character already."

"Tell that to Mom," Natalie groaned, giggling.

"Seriously, Natalie—how are you liking camp? Because I've spoken with your mother, and we both agree that if you're really miserable, you can come home. She says your letters—the few that she's gotten—are written with your typical sarcasm, and she can't make out how bad it really is. So you have to fess up."

"You spoke to Mom?" Natalie asked softly. Accepting as she was of her parents' love lives, a part of her still couldn't quite believe that their marriage was over. They had divorced when she was four, so she'd had some time to get used to it, and she and her mother were happy and doing well. But the fact that the separation had been so . . . *amicable* almost made it harder to accept. If they were screaming and yelling about things like child support all the time, she might be more willing to let go of the fantasy that they'd someday get back together.

"She called last week," Josie chirped, breaking into Natalie's little imaginary tour of the alternate reality where her nuclear family was still intact. "Because she knew we were coming to surprise you."

"Yes, we're all in on it, sweetie. If you're unhappy, we'll take you right home. Well, technically, you'd have to come out to LA, because your mother won't be back from Europe for a few more weeks. But I have about a month before I head off on location again, so the timing would be perfect."

Natalie frowned. She wasn't sure how she felt about it. A week ago, being offered the chance to go home would have been a dream come true. Could it be that so much had changed in such a short period of time? There were things about camp that she could *definitely* do without—spiders in the bathroom, for example. Or that horrible food three times a day. Or having to put up with Chelsea's snipes. But then she thought of smart, sensitive Alyssa, and outgoing Grace. Boisterous Jenna, and energetic Alex. Assuming those girls still planned on talking to her, she couldn't just bail on them. What would Val do in nature without her? Or Simon? *That is, if he doesn't hate me,* Natalie thought.

But if her friends *did* hate her, she knew she had to stay and smooth things over. Going home wasn't the answer. Hannah wasn't in New York City, and Maggie and Ellen were away, too, so what was the fun in that? And as for visiting her father in Los Angeles . . . well, she loved being out in California (she especially loved his huge house and heated swimming pool), but she had already planned a trip to see him at the end of the summer, just before school started. Now was camp time. And to Natalie's surprise, she found that she was determined to stick it out.

"You know what, Dad?" Natalie found herself saying. "It's okay. I've kind of gotten used to camp. I can't walk away now."

Her father grinned, his bright blue eyes twinkling. "What did I tell you? More than enough character! That's what I like to hear, honey. I'm proud of you."

"Me too," Josie echoed, pushing her plate aside and flagging down the waitress. "Do you think they have fat-free frozen yogurt in this place?"

▲ ▲ ▲

"I'm just disappointed that you didn't find anything today that you wanted," Tad said to Natalie. They had finished their lunch and driven back to camp, stopping only at a farm stand on the side of the road. Now his limo was parked just outside the front entrance to camp. Natalie didn't want to risk generating attention by bringing her father back onto the campgrounds. She'd had enough time in the spotlight already that day—and somehow, she had a feeling that she hadn't seen the last of it.

"Not true," Natalie pointed out. "Everyone in my bunk is going to be *really* into the peanut butter and chocolate fudge we got at the farm stand." She grinned devilishly in Josie's direction. "Want to take some home with you? I think it's fat-free."

Josie swatted Natalie playfully. "You're terrible. But he's right, we wanted to bring you stuff."

"Are you kidding? You've got a whole wild retail wonderland stuffed in the trunk!" Natalie's eyes had almost popped out of her head when her father and Josie had shown her their idea of a "care package"—they'd loaded up the car with industrial-sized boxes of cereal, cookies, chips, and soda ("Have you heard of this place called Costco?" Josie had asked, wrinkling her nose with distaste.), as well as CDs, DVDs, books, hair accessories, and more than a few cute T-shirts and skirts. "Trust me," Natalie said, "I've got plenty of stuff."

"Are you *sure* you want us to drop this all off in New York, then?" her father asked doubtfully.

Natalie shrugged uneasily. "The thing is, Dad, some of the kids might think it was weird, me bringing all that stuff in. I mean, that's enough food to carry us through to next summer! I just . . . I really don't want to seem different, you know?"

Her father sighed. "I understand. But if you won't let me spoil you, what have I got left?"

Josie patted his shoulder reassuringly. "You could spoil *me*."

Tad laughed and hugged both of his girls close to him. "All right, then, I guess, if we can't convince you to take this stuff, and we can't convince you to run away with us, then the time has come for us to be on our way. We have a suite booked at the Soho House for tonight, and Josie has a trainer coming early tomorrow morning."

Natalie thought fleetingly of the luxurious Soho House hotel and its rooftop swimming pool. Her father was just one of the many celebrity guests who stayed there, and the pool club was considered a real scene. All she had to do was say the word, and she'd be sipping ice-cold soft drinks on a lounge chair all afternoon. She groaned. "You're killing me, Dad," she said. "But I'll just say good-bye now." She threw her arms around him and gave him a huge hug. "Thanks for stopping by. It was a fantastic surprise."

"You know I'd still love a tour of the camp, kiddo. Especially the famous nature shack."

Natalie groaned. "Haven't you already caused

enough of a stir?"

Her father laughed. "You're right. At least I got to talk to the camp director before I met up with you. And that woman—Kathleen, is that her name? Very energetic woman. And I got that great twenty minutes of quality time on the porch of your bunk. I hope I didn't get you in too much trouble with your friends?" he asked.

"Either that, or I'm going to be *really* popular for the rest of the summer. It could go either way. But whichever it's going to be, I'm going to have to face things sooner rather than later." She squared her shoulders dramatically.

"You're a trooper," her father laughed. He gestured toward the trunk again. "Your things will be waiting for you when you get home in August. Sort of a reward for sticking it out."

Natalie nodded. "Cool. And thanks." She paused and thought for a moment. "Well, maybe I'll just take one box of cookies. And some chips. And soda. You know, for the girls."

Josie nodded knowingly. "The girls deserve it."

"And, um, maybe that really cute tank top with the ribbons on the shoulders."

Josie and Tad smiled. "Do you want to have another look in the trunk before we go?" Tad asked.

Natalie grinned sheepishly. "Well," she said, "if you've brought it all this way . . ."

▲ ▲ ▲

By the time Natalie had finished saying her good-byes to her father and Josie, dinner was long over and the entire camp, it felt like, was off at evening activity. Natalie realized she didn't even know what evening activity was supposed to be that night. She figured maybe it was for the best. She'd return to her bunk, and put away her things. Then maybe she'd have some time to relax before having to face her bunkmates again.

She pushed open the door of her bunk to find Marissa and Pete sitting on Marissa's bed, talking quietly. Natalie had the feeling she was interrupting something. *What's going on between Marissa and Pete?* she wondered. After all, she knew they were friendly.

But if either of them were feeling awkward, they didn't show it. Marissa sat up straight on her bed and beamed at Natalie. "Hey, girl, how was your day with your dad?" she asked.

Natalie blushed. "Oh, you know . . . fun. Unexpected," she said.

Pete smiled. "I'll say!"

"I guess I should have said something," Natalie admitted. She dropped her clothes and books on her bed, and brought a bag of chips over to where Marissa and Pete sat. She popped the bag open and offered them a snack.

"Parents are the best," Pete said, crunching down on a handful of chips.

"My dad's got his issues, but he means well," Natalie agreed.

"He's got great taste in snack food," Marissa said.

Natalie couldn't believe it. Were they really not going to give her a hard time for not coming clean with them about her father? "Okay, so what's the deal?" she demanded abruptly. "Why are you being so normal about this?"

Marissa and Pete glanced at each other briefly, and then back at Natalie. "What would you rather we do?" Marissa asked softly. "It's your family, and it's your business. I think you're a great girl, Natalie, and I respect you. If you didn't want to talk about what your father does, then that's your call. I don't blame you. I bet you have to deal with a lot of weirdness, growing up as Tad Maxwell's daughter."

Natalie felt relief course through her in waves. Leave it to Marissa to be totally understanding. "Exactly," she said. "I didn't mean to lie, I just . . . wanted to spend the summer without having to deal with that. I mean, you never know how people are going to react, and I just wanted to be here on my own terms this summer."

"I totally dig that," Pete said. He reached forward for more chips.

Marissa rolled her eyes. "He's just easily bribed. A little salt and vinegar goes a long way." She suddenly lowered her voice, slightly more serious. "But I think you have to be prepared for the fact that some other people might react a little differently."

"Is everyone mad at me?" Natalie asked nervously. "Not that I blame them. I mean, I sort of lied."

"I don't know that people are 'mad,' Nat, but definitely, some of your friends are going to wonder why you didn't trust them enough to come clean," Marissa replied.

"And then there are others who might just be really weird now that they know who your father is," Pete said. "People react really strangely to fame, you know?"

Natalie sighed heavily. "Actually, I do." She looked up at the two of them. "So where is everybody now?"

"Capture the flag tonight," Marissa explained. "Up in Far Meadow. But it's half over, anyway. You can stay here with us if you want."

"I really appreciate it, Marissa," Natalie said. "But I guess I have to deal sooner or later.

"It might as well be sooner."

▲ ▲ ▲

Natalie could hear the sounds of cheering and laughing long before the sprawl of Far Meadow actually came into view. She wasn't really sure what "capture the flag" was and she didn't much mind having missed half the game. Now, she was almost deliberately dragging her feet. She did and she didn't want to deal with her fellow campers just yet.

Rounding the corner, she could see Alex in a huddle with Sarah, Brynn, Valerie, and Alyssa. She broke into a jog and ran over to where they stood.

"Can someone fill me in on what this game is about?" she asked, trying to sound more confident than she felt.

Everybody jumped. "Nat!" Alex said. She looked startled, and it was obvious that she was making a deliberate effort to compose herself. "Hey," she said coolly. "Did you have fun with your dad?"

Natalie nodded. "Well, you know, it was a big surprise. It's always a surprise to see him." She tried desperately to catch Alyssa's eye, but her friend just looked away.

The rest of the girls all nodded in unison, as though they understood. To Natalie, the moment seemed to occur in slow-motion, and it felt very awkward. But if no one was going to say anything, then she wouldn't, either.

"Natalie!"

Natalie turned to see Chelsea sprinting toward her as though they were long lost friends. "Are you on our team?" she asked breathlessly. Her tank top was streaked with grass stains and a few blond wisps had escaped her ponytail, but if anything, the flush in her cheeks made her look even prettier than usual. "We've got a no-lose strategy. Did Alex fill you in?"

Alex shrugged. "I didn't have a chance yet."

Natalie's head was spinning. The scene felt almost completely surreal. Her friends were being polite but awkward, and Chelsea was suddenly her bestest best friend in the world? This was so not what she wanted! *This* was why she hadn't wanted to let people know who her father was!

Chelsea leaned in again. "Look, Betsey is our offense." She gestured to midfield where a lanky brunette from 3A hunkered, hands on her knees. "Jenna's gonna create a distraction—see? Bennett's playing defense, so Jenna's on top of him. Then Betsey will go long and grab the flag. We'll go wait just outside of the goal zone, and once she's got the flag, she'll pass. Then we can run it back to our side."

Natalie stared at Chelsea in disbelief. "I'm, uh, not such a fast runner." To say the least.

Chelsea burst out laughing and gave Natalie a playful shove. "Come on. It's fine." She grabbed Natalie's arm and began to drag her upfield. "All you have to do is act like you know what you're doing."

"You guys—" Natalie protested, and glanced fleetingly at Alex.

"It's a solid strategy," Alex said, wrapping her glossy black hair back into a sloppy ponytail. "Go for it."

The girls ran up the meadow, Chelsea pausing to high-five Betsey behind her back. Once they were within spitting distance of the other team's goal, Chelsea shoved Natalie hard. "Go distract the goalies."

"Huh?" Natalie asked as she stumbled forward. Three boys stood in front of the goal, which she assumed was where the flag would be. One was Jenna's brother Adam, and one was a boy named Caleb who was on the newspaper with Natalie.

One was Simon.

Before Natalie could even begin to think of what to say to him, Caleb was in her face, growling and pretending to be tough. "Don't even think about it, girlie," he said, puffing his chest out and standing really close to her. "We're all over this flag."

"Dude, do you know who her father is?" Adam asked. "Tad Maxwell. You know, huge action spy. She might be able to kick your butt!"

"It's just a movie," Natalie said desperately. She looked over at Simon, but he wasn't looking back. "I mean, he's really not that tough."

"Oh, yeah?" Caleb asked thoughtfully. "I've got an idea. How about you hook me up? I get to meet your dad, you get to capture the flag?" He winked and then burst out laughing as though this were the most hysterical joke ever told.

"You know who I want to meet? Josie McLaughlan!" Adam said. "Her father's girlfriend. She's so hot, I could cry. Do you think she'll come up for Visiting Day, Natalie?"

"I doubt it," Natalie said. "I think my father's going to be shooting." *Do we have to talk about this?* she thought anxiously.

"But you could get us, like, an autograph or something, right?" Caleb pressed.

"Ah, sure, maybe," Natalie said. Out of the corner of her eye, she could see Chelsea creeping behind the flag, waiting for Morgan from 3B to break in and away. She was racking her brain for the right thing to say to Simon but drawing a blank. It didn't matter—he didn't look like he wanted to talk, anyway.

Suddenly, Betsey burst forward, cutting between Natalie and Caleb in a blur of long brown braid and legs. She snatched the flag from its pole and circled around Simon, passing it off to Chelsea and backing away again.

"YEAH!" Chelsea screamed, tearing forward and making a break for the far end of the field.

"Dude, are you asleep?" Caleb shouted to Simon, taking off after Chelsea. After a moment, Adam followed him. Now Natalie stood alone, facing Simon. The tension in the air was thick. A thousand ways to open a conversation raced through Natalie's mind, but she rejected them all.

Finally, Simon spoke. "You should go after them," he said quietly.

Then he ran off to follow his teammates.

chapter
ELEVEN

"Nat, do you want to borrow my extra flashlight for the camping trip?"

Natalie looked up to find Chelsea beaming down at her, waving a bright yellow flashlight. "Oh, ah, I've got my own," she managed. "But, thanks." She pressed her toiletries case into her daypack and zipped it shut. Everyone who was going on the camping trip had packed a larger duffel that was being driven to the campsite separately. That baggage had been delivered to the rec hall the night before. But all the campers were responsible for bringing their own daypacks and carrying them on the hike.

"Do you have enough bug repellant? I have two bottles," Chelsea offered. "And also sunscreen."

"It's okay, Chelsea," Natalie insisted, trying her hardest not to sound testy. "I'm all set." She knew Chelsea was just trying to be nice—well, she assumed so, anyway—but the girl was starting to drive her crazy. Most of Natalie's friends had been remote and aloof since yesterday. And for her part, Natalie didn't know how to behave around them, either. But not Chelsea. Chelsea had been all buddy-buddy on the way back from evening activity the night before, and now she was practically trying to pack Natalie's bag for her. Meanwhile, everyone else in the bunk was tiptoeing around her, and all the other campers were acting like she was some kind of rock goddess. Natalie felt like she was losing her mind. She couldn't believe it, but she was almost looking forward to the camping trip! At least it would help her get away from everything and clear her mind. When she was back home and feeling stressed-out, she always went for long walks in Central Park. This camping trip was the closest she was going to get to that for at least six more weeks.

"All right," she said to no one in particular. "I've got to go. I'm in charge of picking up the lunches for the group and bringing them to the rec hall. That's where the van is meeting us." She shouldered her backpack. "Chelsea, Valerie, I'll meet you there. Good-bye, everyone! Wish me luck avoiding snakebites!"

Her bunkmates laughed and offered vague reassurances. None of it was especially comforting.

Natalie started out toward the mess hall for the lunches. She hadn't gotten farther than the front porch, though, when she heard the door creak open and bang shut again behind her. "Nat, wait," she heard. She stopped walking.

It was Alyssa. "Look, I'm sorry I've been avoiding you," she said, biting her lip. "I feel terrible." Alyssa hadn't exactly been rude to Natalie, but she definitely hadn't been overly friendly the evening before. Natalie had tried to convince herself that it was because of Alyssa's deep-seated aversion to capture the flag, but inside she knew better. Which was probably why she herself had been reluctant to approach her friend. She just wasn't sure what to say.

"*You* feel terrible?" Natalie cried in disbelief. "Are you kidding me? I'm the one who lied to you guys! I feel awful! I wouldn't blame you if you never wanted to speak to me again!"

"Of course I want to speak to you again," Alyssa said. "Listen, you have the right to want to keep certain things secret. God knows, I haven't told you everything about my crazy family. Just wait until we're back home in the fall, and you meet my older sister. What a freak *she* is!"

Natalie giggled. "I guess everyone's family is a little bit nuts."

"Excuse me, but have you *seen* Jenna when she and Adam bicker? It's like they're possessed or something. Anyway, I don't blame you. Especially now that half the people in camp are your biggest fans. I can totally get why you wanted to keep this quiet. It must be so annoying to feel like no one knows the real you."

"Exactly!" Natalie said, relieved that her friend understood.

"But I never knew anyone who was famous before, and when I saw who your father was, I guess I flipped," Alyssa continued softly. "I mean, you're so pretty and funny and sophisticated—you're from New York, after all. So I knew you were definitely a character."

"Why does everyone keep telling me how much character I have?" Natalie asked wryly. "It could really give a girl a complex."

"Will you shut up and let me finish?" Alyssa asked. "Character, I like. But when it started to seem like maybe you had this whole alternate-Hollywood lifestyle or something, I got nervous. Like maybe I wasn't cool enough for you anymore." She looked down at the ground as though maybe she thought she'd said too much.

Natalie's eyes flew open. "Okay, first of all, I am *so* not more sophisticated than you! You've read, like, every book *ever*, and you have the coolest taste in music! And you draw so well, and you're the best writer on the paper! And second of all, most of my friends in New York are really, really normal. Maybe some of them have money, but they don't go riding around in limos everywhere. That's just my father. And if you want the truth, well . . . I don't see him that often. I mean, he means well. I know he loves me. But he's pretty involved in his own thing. So if you think my life is one big Hollywood party after another, well . . . you have no idea. Honestly? I spend most of the time watching TV at home with my friends." She crossed her arms in front of her chest and regarded her friend. "Okay?"

Alyssa nodded, clearly glad to have everything out in the open. "Okay. Can we stop being idiots now? Because yesterday when we weren't talking was really bad."

Natalie smiled. "You're telling me? *Chelsea* is, like, my new best friend!"

"Ha ha," Alyssa said. "Have fun on the camping trip!"

"Very funny," Natalie said, making a face. She glanced at her watch. "Now I *really* have to go," she said. "Can't keep the poison ivy waiting."

▲ ▲ ▲

"What are in these lunches, anyway?" Pete asked, pretending to struggle under the weight of the garbage bag he was carrying. He and Marissa had been in the mess hall when Natalie came by, and they had packed up the lunches for her, offering to help her carry them to the rec hall.

"So, Nat," Marissa said, "how was everyone last night?"

"Pretty much what I expected," Natalie said. "Half the girls in our bunk have no idea how to act around me. Like Alex and Brynn and Sarah. They're behaving like robots. Very polite, stiff robots."

"What about the other half?" Marissa asked.

"Oh, they're really into me now that they know who my father is. All fake-nice and stuff."

As if on cue, Chelsea stepped out in front of them. "Hey, guys!" she said. "Need help?"

Pete stifled a chuckle. "I think we're good, Chelsea. Are you all ready for the camping trip?"

"Totally!" she said. She looked the part, too. She had done her hair up into two cute braids down either side of her head, and she was wearing a crisp white tank top and lightweight cargo capris. Her trail shoes looked appropriately broken-in, and a disposable camera peeked out from one pocket.

"Chelsea, why don't you show Pete where to bring the food," Marissa suggested.

"Totally!" Chelsea repeated. Her enthusiasm was slightly scary.

Marissa poked Natalie in the ribs as they watched the two make their way into the mess hall. "Okay, I can see what you mean," she said.

"Right?" Natalie asked. "I get that all the time. I just didn't want to have to deal with it here. This place was supposed to be a whole new experience."

"Well, I think it's safe to say it *was* a whole new experience, right?" Marissa said. "I mean, look at you. When you first got here, you wouldn't shower without wearing your bathing suit."

"Let's not exaggerate," Natalie protested.

"Almost," Marissa insisted. "And now you're going on a camping trip! In the actual wilderness! Nat, you should really be proud of yourself."

"I guess I sort of am," Natalie admitted. She never liked to say those kinds of things out loud for fear of people thinking she was stuck-up, but in this case, it was definitely true.

"And I think you should know," Marissa continued, "that your true friends are going to stick by you no matter what. Whatever you did or didn't tell them, or whoever your father is, they'll still be on your side. That's how you know they're your friends."

"You're right," Natalie said, thinking of Alyssa. Then she remembered the look on Simon's face just before he ran off after the flag. At least, I hope you are."

▲ ▲ ▲

"Okay, I want you all to line up, boy-girl-boy-girl," Roseanne shouted. She seemed to have forgotten how to speak at a normal decibel today. Of course,

Natalie had to give her credit for dragging a group of fifteen immature eleven-year-olds into the woods overnight with only LJ from the kitchen as support. The line snapped into place and Natalie found herself at the end of it, behind Chelsea, due to an uneven number of boys and girls. "Now I want you to break off into pairs," Roseanne continued. "The person you pair off with is your buddy. No matter where we are or what you're doing, you are always responsible for your buddy. Do you understand? That means *always* knowing where your buddy is and what he or she is doing. The woods aren't dangerous, but we all have to be alert at all times. Devon, Eric, you're buddies," she said, pointing to the first boy-girl combo at the front of the line. Dutifully, the rest of the campers began to partner up.

Natalie glanced down the line. *Paige and Eric*, she ticked off mentally, *Shari and Ross, Michael and Valerie, Topher and Melanie, Brian and Lizzie, Seth and Adrianne* . . . with a sinking feeling, she realized who the threesome would be. After all, there were only three of them left.

Simon and Chelsea . . . and me.

▲ ▲ ▲

Natalie didn't know which was worse, the chafe of her backpack against her shoulders, or the deafening silence between Simon and herself. Both were extremely irritating and slightly painful. And both showed little signs of letting up anytime soon.

Fortunately, Chelsea was doing enough chattering for the both of them. She had, thankfully, taken it upon herself to play the role of group leader. Each pair (or, in their case, trio) was responsible for identifying and gathering several types of flora and fauna along the way. The idea was that they would all share their findings around the campfire that night. Natalie was more open-minded about this trip than she would ever have dreamed, true, but try though she might, she just couldn't get jazzed over rocks, leaves, and twigs for show-and-tell. So it was a good thing that Chelsea was eager to pick up the slack. "Pine needles are so totally obvious," she was saying, waving her map in front of her buddies. She was either completely oblivious to the awkward tension coursing through the air, or deliberately ignoring it. "We totally lucked out."

Natalie frowned at the path beneath her feet, and kicked at a rock. "Totally," she echoed.

"Have you seen any?" Chelsea asked. "'Cause I just haven't yet. But I know we will." She stopped short, tossing her head so her braids flew back over her shoulders dramatically. "Let's take a picture."

"Oh, uh, now?" Natalie asked with alarm. They'd been hiking along at the tail end of the group for about an hour now, Natalie imagining entire conversations with Simon in her head. It didn't seem quite the right time for a Kodak moment. "Why don't you wait until we hit the campsite? Roseanne says there are amazing views."

"Well, duh, I'll take pictures then, too!" Chelsea said, speaking as though Natalie were five years old. "Oh, look—" she squealed. "A rabbit!"

Sure enough, a tiny spotted rabbit leaped out from the trees and landed just before Chelsea's feet. It froze, blinking furiously. Then it hopped away.

"Oh, I *so* need a picture of that!" Chelsea

exclaimed, darting off after it. The rabbit bounced off to the left of the path and down a sloping hill.

Natalie glanced up ahead to where Roseanne and the group were continuing along. Everyone in the group was busy collecting samples from the trail and didn't seem to have noticed that Natalie, Simon, and Chelsea were lagging behind. Suddenly, Natalie felt nervous. They really weren't supposed to go off on their own. But then again, she and Simon were Chelsea's buddies. They couldn't let her out of their sight. That was the rules.

"Shoot," she muttered. "What should we do?"

Simon looked equally panicked, in his own low-key way. "I guess we have to go after her, pull her back," he said.

They took one last, fleeting glance at the group and started down the slope after Chelsea. "Chelsea, come on!" Natalie shouted. "We're not supposed to go off the path!"

"Don't be such a freak, Nat!" Chelsea called back over her shoulder. "We've barely been gone five minutes! Come on! The rabbit's trying to hide! It would make a really cute picture."

"If the rabbit is hiding, Chelsea, it's probably scared of you," Simon pointed out. He slid a few paces and skidded to a stop in front of her.

"*Uf,*" Natalie grunted, tripping over her feet and landing inches behind Simon. She grabbed at him for traction then pulled back as if she'd been electrocuted. "Sorry."

She blew a thick clump of hair off her face gracelessly. "Where's Thumper?"

"You scared him off," Chelsea snapped, suddenly

cranky. "Thanks a lot."

"Um, sorry?" Natalie said. "I practically skidded down the hill on my butt. It was hardly on purpose." She was hot and tired and not in the mood for attitude. "Anyway, you know we're not supposed to run off." She rubbed at her shoulders and thought absently that it was probably time to reapply the sunscreen.

"Guys," Simon said, breaking into the heated moment. "Forget the rabbit. I think we have other problems."

Natalie put her hands on her hips. "What?" she asked. It was humid, buggy, and they still had at least another hour to go before they reached the campsite. What other problems could there possibly be?

He jerked his head back in the direction of the group. "Well, for starters, I don't see them anymore," he said.

Natalie glanced over to where he was pointing. He was right. She couldn't make out even the faintest forms on the path. She had no idea where the rest of the group had gone.

They were on their own.

"I *knew* I shouldn't have paired up with Miss New York," Chelsea grumbled, trudging along. Since they had gotten separated from the group, she had completely reverted back to her old self. She was sour and angry, taking constant jabs at Natalie. It was as though her whole about-face thing had never happened at all.

For her part, Natalie was mostly exhausted and

exasperated, and more than ready to meet up with the group again to set up camp. "Yeah, yeah, I know," Natalie muttered. "You're my best friend, too, Chelsea. Look, for now, let's just concentrate on finding Roseanne. I never thought I'd say this, but I'm dying to set up the cooker and roll out our sleeping bags. I'd even be willing to bathe in the river." She stopped for a moment, having a thought. "The river!" she said excitedly.

Chelsea glared at her. "Yeah? What about it?"

"Roseanne said we were camping a quarter mile upstream from where the river forked." Flustered, she pulled the map out of her back pocket. It was damp and sticky, like everything else, but she ignored that and unfolded it. "Here's where we last saw the group," she said, pointing to a spot on the dirt path. "That's where we went when we saw the rabbit—I think." She slid her finger down and off to one side. "But I think we thought we were going parallel, but really, we veered off west. And the river is north."

Simon peered at the map over her shoulder. "I think you're right."

"So what does that mean?" Chelsea demanded.

"It means if we head north again, we'll find the river," Simon explained.

"—and if we find the river, we'll find the group," Natalie finished.

"Why should I listen to you two, anyway?" Chelsea whined. "Natalie, you're just a stuck-up city girl, anyway. *Not* exactly the ideal trail guide!" She smirked to herself at her own nasty joke.

"Why should you listen to me?" Natalie asked. "Because if it weren't for *you*, we wouldn't be in this mess, anyway! Now come on—we don't have time for this. What other choice do we have?"

"Ugh, *fine*," Chelsea agreed. "But I don't trust you at all."

"I can live with that," Natalie said. She fished a compass out of her backpack. "Simon, can you read this thing?"

He took it from her and held it flat in his palm. "Yup," he said. "Follow me."

"*Natalie!*"

Natalie thought she had never in her life been so glad to hear the sound of Roseanne's voice. For her part, Roseanne sounded thrilled beyond belief to see Natalie, Simon, and Chelsea.

"*Where* did you guys get off to? We've got LJ driving the van off in every direction trying to find you."

"Well, obviously not *every* direction," Natalie quipped wearily. "Have you got any water?" She tossed her pack off her back and collapsed down next to it, taking her hair out of its ponytail and shaking it out.

"Of course, of course," Roseanne said, offering her canteen to Natalie. "The others are pitching the tents over in that clearing—" she pointed to a spot in the distance. "And then when LJ gets back, he's going to start cooking dinner."

"Thank God," Natalie said. "I dropped my granola bar in the river a mile or so back, and I'm starving."

"Whatever," Chelsea interrupted. "It's totally Natalie's fault that we got lost."

"What? But—" Natalie began, then stopped. She was too tired, anyway.

"Chelsea, dear, why don't you go help the others pitch the tents, okay?" Roseanne suggested. Chelsea marched off in the direction indicated without offering even a second glance at Natalie or Simon.

Once she was out of earshot, Natalie turned to Roseanne imploringly. "It is so *not* my fault that we got lost—" she started.

Roseanne laughed. "Why do I not doubt that? Sweetie, don't get yourself all worked up. You've had a long afternoon. Just relax and take a load off. Simon can fill me in on the rest."

Natalie had to admit, the idea of resting for a bit sounded awfully appealing. From across the clearing, she could hear the laughter of the group. The thought of making conversation and explaining what happened felt overwhelming. A moment to regroup seemed like the right thing. And regardless of where their friendship was, she trusted Simon to relay the truth to Roseanne. So she smiled at the both of them, stood, brushed herself off, and walked away—though not *too* far away. She'd learned her lesson, after all.

Natalie found a quiet spot in the shade. She crouched on a flat rock and looked out over the hilltops. She could see the river down below—and if she turned around, she could see the other campers chilling out at the site. She exhaled deeply and took in the scenery.

Central Park had nothing to compare to this. True, she could ride horseback or canoe in the lake, eat ice cream or watch Shakespeare performed outdoors. New York was a special place, no doubt about it. But then, so was Lakeview. Natalie realized that she didn't care that Chelsea was being bratty again—in a way, it was even a relief. At least it felt natural. And she would somehow apologize to Simon. Even if he didn't want to be friends, she owed him that much, and she would gather up the courage to tell him so. But not now. Right now, she was just going to breathe in the clean mountain air.

I'm like a commercial for Grape-Nuts or something, she realized with wonder. *What's going on with me? Am I, like, a real camper now?* She glanced down at her legs. The scratches and bruises she'd gotten while trying to link up with the rest of the group were proof-positive that she was definitely gaining a new perspective on the great outdoors. The thought made her smile to herself.

"I've got something that'll *really* make you smile," she heard.

She looked up to see Simon holding out a granola bar. "Since I knew you lost yours."

She took it eagerly. "Have I mentioned I'm *dying* of hunger?" she asked.

He gave her a look. "I think once or twice."

She swatted at him jokingly. "Sit. Share," she commanded.

Simon lowered himself onto the ground next to her and took half of the granola bar willingly. "So," he started, suddenly sounding nervous.

"No, me first," Natalie cut in. "I need to tell you that I'm sorry. I'm sorry I didn't say anything about my father. I shouldn't have been so secretive. And I'm sorry I ran away the other day. I could tell you were upset, and I just wasn't ready to deal."

Simon nodded thoughtfully. "I know. I get it. I

mean, I'm not gonna lie—I was really upset yesterday, Nat. It really hurt me to think that you didn't feel you could tell me."

"It's not that—" Natalie started.

"—listen," Simon pressed. "The point is, I get it now. I saw how everyone reacted to your father, and I can see why you wanted to keep it a secret for a while."

"I wanted people to like me for who I am," Natalie explained.

"People?" Simon asked.

Natalie blushed. "Some people more than others."

Simon put his arm around Natalie's shoulders. Rockets went off in her stomach. "I just hope that from now on, you know you can always be straight with me."

Natalie tilted her head to look him straight in the eyes. "I know. I will. I promise."

"I think you were awesome today, the way you knew how to find the way back to camp," he said.

"Come on—you knew, too."

"You had the compass. We would have been lost without you," Simon said.

"Fair enough," Natalie agreed. "Let's just compromise and say that we're a great team."

Simon slipped his hand around Natalie's own. "Absolutely," he said.

chapter

TWELVE

"Okay, so is it true that Chelsea was, like, trapped by a bear and almost eaten?" Brynn asked. She sounded sort of excited at the prospect.

"Not even!" Natalie exclaimed. "Where did you hear such a thing?"

"Well, Simon's telling everyone how you rescued Chelsea after she got lost," Alex said.

The three girls were on their way out of the mess hall following dinner. Natalie and the rest of the campers from the overnight had returned back to Lakeview early that afternoon, but they were given a few hours to kick back and do whatever they wanted. For Natalie, that meant sitting out on the front porch of 3C reading *Entertainment Weekly*. She only counted two wild rumors connected to her father. To her that was progress. One said he was having hair transplants done before his next movie. To the best of her knowledge, Natalie's father had never had any plastic surgery done. She'd have to make sure and give him a hard time about that gossip the next time they spoke.

Since Natalie had spent the afternoon by herself, she was totally unaware of the rumors that were flying around camp about *her*. Simon had let it slip—intentionally, she guessed—that the three of them had been separated from the group and had been forced to find their way to the campsite with little more than a compass and some bug spray. But somehow, the story had morphed into a tale of daring rescue. One that made her sound like a cross between Lara Croft and the Crocodile Hunter. It was too funny. She had to admit, she didn't mind the attention that much. It seemed to have superceded people's obsession with her movie-star father, so for now, at least, she was okay with it.

"It was so not a big deal," Natalie said, shaking her head. "Chelsea ran off, and we ran after her." It was the truth, after all.

Chelsea had been quiet since they'd all returned. Those who were talking about her didn't seem to have the guts to go right up *to* her and ask her about the trip. She and the rest of bunk 3C were still milling outside of the mess hall while Brynn, Alex, and Natalie killed time in the nearby pagoda. Natalie was finding that her opinion toward Alex had mellowed slightly. The girl was definitely a type-A model camper, but she was friendly and sincere, and she was one of the few of Natalie's bunkmates who had really gone out of her way to be as normal as possible after she found out the truth about Natalie's father.

"Well, I heard that when she realized that you guys had lost the rest of the group, she totally freaked, and you had to, like, talk her down," Brynn said.

She seemed pretty unwilling to entertain any other version of the story, and Natalie decided she wasn't too interested in correcting her, after all. It *had* been a pretty harrowing experience, and she deserved at least some of the glory, didn't she? "Someone had to step up," she said airily.

"Tell us, Nat, how does it feel to have barely escaped from the wilderness with your life?" Alex asked jokingly. She held out an imaginary microphone, pretending to be a newscaster.

"No comment," Natalie said, cracking up. She saw Marissa talking to Pete, Brian, and Beth, and she ran over to them.

"Hey!" Marissa said, smiling. "You made it out alive."

Natalie groaned. "Just barely."

"Yeah, so we heard," Pete teased. "Aren't you glad all those hours in the nature shack finally paid off?"

"Ahem," Brian interjected. "I believe it was her excellent training during sports that prepared her for the physical challenges of her outdoor adventure."

"Definitely," Natalie agreed, laughing.

"Too bad she *still* won't go into the water for free swim!" Beth protested.

"Excuse me, but after my harrowing experience, shouldn't I get a get-out-of-jail-free card?" Natalie asked.

"Fair enough," Beth conceded.

"We heard that Chelsea, ah, isn't recovering quite as well," Pete said delicately.

"Well, she wasn't exactly thinking positively when we got lost," Natalie said, thinking back to how incredibly negative she herself had been when she got to camp. She actually felt a little bit sorry for Chelsea. Now that they were back, no one had a good word to say about her. "But, I mean, it was a hard day. It was hot, and we were tired—and we had *no* idea where we were going. I was just crossing my fingers that the compass was going to work. I can't really blame her for being suspicious."

"Oh, gosh, Nat, that's so *generous* of you," hissed a voice in her ear.

Natalie turned to find Chelsea shooting her a look of death. The girl had obviously overheard the entire exchange. "No, Chelsea, we were just—" Natalie began.

"—Like I care," Chelsea spat, and stormed off.

"Yikes," Pete said, raising an eyebrow.

"But, well . . . I guess at least things are back to normal?" Marissa asked, shrugging tentatively.

"Exactly," Natalie agreed. "And you know what? You were right."

"What about?" Marissa asked, puzzled.

At that moment, Alyssa emerged from the mess hall, notebook tucked under one arm and black hair piled up on the top of her head. She squinted into the sunlight, then spotted Natalie and smiled, making her way over to her friend.

"Hey there, superstar," she said, tossing an arm around Natalie's shoulder. "Let's get going."

"You were the one that told me, Marissa—that my true friends would always stick by me," Natalie said, sticking out her tongue at Alyssa. "And you were right."

▲ ▲ ▲

"Trauma-rama or horoscopes?" Julie asked, waving two magazines in the air by way of comparison.

"Oooh, horoscopes," Jenna said. "I need to know whether or not—" she stopped abruptly.

"What?" Julie asked, narrowing her gaze. "What have you got planned, my little terror?"

"Nothing," Jenna sang innocently. "Nothing at all."

"Trauma-rama," Natalie put in. "Do they have one where, like, this city girl goes off to this weird place in the country where kids voluntarily sleep on threadbare mattresses and pee in beaten-up, bug-infested stalls, and then after almost two weeks of pretending she isn't the hugest fish out of water, her big movie-star father shows up and outs her as a Hollywood brat?"

"Um, no, that one's not in here, Nat," Julie said sarcastically. "But have you got something on your mind?"

"First things first," Natalie said, reaching under her bed and sliding out the economy-sized box of cookies. "Snacks."

"Natalie, you know you're supposed to tell us what you've got and clear it before giving it out," Julie said, pretending to be more annoyed than she was.

"Do you want one?" Natalie asked knowingly.

"Actually, I kind of want two," Julie admitted, scooting over to the box. "Okay, ladies, we'll have a little extended evening activity before lights-out. Courtesy of Natalie."

"Courtesy of Tad Maxwell," Natalie said. "You are eating cookies purchased by Tad Maxwell."

"That's a very tough offer to turn down," Alex said, pretending to swoon. But Nat noticed she passed the box without taking any cookies.

"Or, at least purchased by his assistant," Natalie amended. "My dad can get a little busy."

"I'll bet!" Grace said.

"I owe you all an apology," Natalie said, growing serious for a moment. "I didn't mean to lie. Or omit. Or whatever. I just really wanted to have a chance to get to know you all without having the thing with my father be a part of it. I mean, I wanted you to like me on my own terms."

"Well, come on, that would never be an issue," Grace said. " 'Cause of how we don't really like you, anyway." She grinned to show that she was teasing and reached for another cookie. "Hey, does anyone have anything to drink?"

"My dad also brought me some sodas," Natalie said, feeling slightly embarrassed. "I guess sometimes he goes overboard."

"Hey, when it comes to Diet Pepsi, he can go as overboard as he wants!" Valerie said. "Maybe now I'll even go see his next movie!"

"I have an idea for lights-out," Karen suggested quietly. Everyone turned to stare at her. She almost never spoke out in large groups. "How about Natalie tells us some good Hollywood dirt? That's better than anything you read in a magazine, because we know it's real."

"Oh, I don't know," Natalie hedged . . . But then she stopped herself. *Why not?* she thought. *It's not like they don't read all about him in* People *magazine every day. And since I've been keeping my dad a secret, I haven't been able to dish about him since I got here.* "Cool, I'm in!" she decided. The girls whooped and cheered.

"Hey, the first two weeks are almost up and we have to pick our next electives," Alex reminded everyone. "Does anyone have any idea what they want?"

"Ceramics," Chelsea said sullenly. "I guess I'll take

ceramics and drama."

"Photography!" Jenna said. "And maybe wood-working."

"I really want to stay on the newspaper," Alyssa said. "I'll have to think about what else I want to do."

"I wish they offered an elective for napping," Grace quipped. "That or eating." She stuffed another cookie into her mouth for good measure.

"What about you, Nat?" Sarah asked. "Are you and Simon gonna, like, pick your free periods together?" she teased.

Natalie laughed, feeling a little flustered. "Um, not quite," she stammered.

"So is he your *boyfriend* now, or what?" Grace sang, kissing the back of her hand furiously in a bizarre imitation of, Natalie assumed, her and Simon.

Natalie shrugged. "I don't know. He's my friend. And he's a boy. And maybe he's also a little bit more than a friend. But I've never really had a boyfriend before, and I don't know what that means."

"Translated, that means she *likes* him, likes him," Alyssa translated, smiling at her friend.

"Ugh, *gross*," Karen said, echoing the sentiment of all the bunkmates. Everyone erupted into a chorus of, "eew," and, "barf," and Brynn leaned over and made hearty retching noises.

"Enough, people," Marissa broke in. "Trust me— soon enough, you won't be thinking that boys are all that gross."

"Boys like Pete?" Natalie asked. "Or other boys?"

"*Any* boys," Marissa confirmed, dodging the question skillfully. "And anyway, Nat, you never answered the question. What electives are you gonna go for next?"

Natalie scrunched up her face as if in deep concentration. "You know? I think I'll stick with nature," she joked.

Her bunkmates cracked up and pelted her with their pillows. Natalie found herself laughing, too. She couldn't believe that just two weeks into the summer, she'd already made some amazing friends and a maybe-boyfriend—and survived overnight in the woods. She had no intention of taking nature again—and she knew Julie would say she'd already paid her dues. So now she could try anything else she wanted. Even something she'd never done before. Something that could be hard or scary or different. Something that she might not even be good at.

No matter what, Natalie knew she was ready. After two weeks at Camp Lakeview, she could handle anything that came at her. And more than that?

She'd probably even enjoy herself, too.

Turn the page for a sneak preview of

camp
CONFIDENTIAL

Jenna's Dilemma

available now!

chapter

FOUR

"Okay, Jenna, what scares you the most about diving?" Marissa asked as she, Jenna, and Alex stood on the edge of the beginner's pier again that afternoon.

"Everything," Jenna replied.

"It can't be *everything*," Alex said, crossing her arms over her chest.

"Okay, fine. I just don't get how you're supposed to go headfirst," Jenna said, gesturing toward the water. "The water is so far down. And doesn't it hurt?"

"It totally doesn't," Alex said. "You just need to do it."

Jenna was starting to get tense with Alex breathing down her neck. It seemed like her idea of helping Jenna was to stand there telling her to just do it. She was like a walking, talking Nike ad. It was a good thing Marissa had offered to help. If the CIT hadn't been there, Jenna probably would have given up by now.

"Okay, how about this?" Marissa said. "Why don't you try jumping into the water feetfirst? You can do that, right?"

"Everyone can do that," Jenna said with a scoff, stepping to the edge.

Marissa reached out and touched her arm before she could jump. "But this time, I want you to pay attention to your feet. Really think about how your feet feel when they hit the water, okay?"

Jenna blinked. Think about her feet? Was Marissa losing it? "Um . . . okay," she said.

She jumped off the platform, closed her eyes, and concentrated on her feet. They hit the water, Jenna felt the splash, and then went under. The water rushed up around her, refreshing and cool. Jenna smiled as she swam back up to the surface. She really did love to swim. If only she could just avoid the diving.

"Well?" Marissa asked.

"Well what?" Jenna replied, paddling over to the ladder.

"Did it hurt? Did your feet hurt when they hit the water?" Marissa asked.

Jenna paused as she climbed, thinking about it. "No."

"So if it doesn't hurt your feet when they go in first, it's not going to hurt your head, especially when your hands are breaking the water first," Marissa said happily.

"Wow. She's good," Alex said.

Jenna couldn't have agreed more. Marissa definitely had a point. Why would diving hurt any more than jumping?

"Okay, but what if I hit a rock?" Jenna asked, pulling her wet bathing suit away from her stomach to make the sucking sound she loved and then letting it go.

"Did you even hit the bottom of the lake when you jumped in just now?" Marissa asked.

Jenna felt her face flush slightly. "Um . . . no."

"Well then you're not going to hit it when you dive," Marissa told her. "Besides, there are no rocks down there. It's all sand."

"Swear?" Jenna asked.

"Cross my heart and hope to never wear eyeliner again," Marissa said. She crossed her heart with her finger and held up a flat hand like a Girl Scout.

"And for her, that's serious," Alex said.

Marissa and Jenna laughed, and Jenna walked to the edge of the platform once more, looking down. Suddenly, the water didn't seem as far away. Her stomach was still full of nervous butterflies, but for the first time, she felt like she might actually be able to do this. Marissa had done it when she was scared. Even Alex had told her that she had been a little frightened on her first dive. If they could both do it, why couldn't she?

Jenna turned to Marissa and Alex with a smile. "Okay! I think I'm gonna—"

"Hey, Marissa!"

Jenna's face fell when she saw her sister Stephanie walking the planks toward them. She was wearing her new pink tankini and her hair was back in a perfect French braid.

"Hold that thought, J," Marissa said.

"What are you guys doing out here?" Stephanie asked, slipping on her Hollywood-style tinted sunglasses.

"We're helping Jenna with her diving," Alex announced.

Stephanie looked at Jenna sympathetically. "Oh, yeah, I heard about that, Boo." She stepped over and gathered Jenna's hair behind her head, running her fingers through it like Jenna's mother always did when Jenna was sad. Who did Stephanie think she was, Jenna's personal babysitter? This whole mothering thing was worse than ever this summer. "Anything I can do?" Stephanie asked. She stuck out her bottom lip slightly like she was talking to a pouting baby.

"Yeah. Stop calling me Boo," Jenna replied, stepping out of her sister's grasp.

"Oh, right! Sorry!" Stephanie said with a quick smile. She didn't actually seem sorry at all. "Listen, can I borrow Marissa for a sec? It's kind of important."

"Sure," Jenna said, mostly because Stephanie was already dragging Marissa aside.

"So, we *need* to talk about the social," Stephanie said.

"I know!" Marissa said. "We have to decide on wardrobe, makeup, and, most importantly—"

"Guys!" Marissa and Stephanie said at the same time, then giggled like a couple of crazy people.

Jenna and Alex looked at each other and rolled their eyes. It seemed like all the older girls talked about was which boys they liked and which boys liked them. Didn't they know there were about a million more important things in life? Like the fact that five seconds ago, Jenna had been ready to announce that she was going to take her first dive. Marissa was helping her with the most embarrassing problem of her life, and Stephanie had stolen Marissa away. To talk about what? Stupid boys!

I'm never going to be able to dive now, Jenna thought, staring down at the water sadly. The moment of confidence had passed. She was back to being petrified. What had she been thinking?

"Don't look now, but here comes your uglier half," Alex joked.

Ugh! Could things get any worse? Adam, Simon, Natalie, and Chelsea were all walking toward them, and Adam had that look on his face. That superior look he always got when he was feeling proud of himself about something. What had he done now, dove off the high dive?

Simon, Nat, and Chelsea stopped a few feet away to chat with Alex, and Adam joined Jenna at the edge of the pier.

"Hey, Jen," Adam said. "Why so bummed?"

"Stephanie," Jenna grumbled, glaring at her sister and Marissa over her shoulder. "Marissa was helping me out, and Stephanie came over, and now it's like I'm invisible."

"You could never be invisible!" Adam said. "Especially not in that bathing suit," he added with a laugh, eyeing her yellow-and-pink Hawaiian print tank.

"Shut up!" Jenna shot back.

"Okay! Okay!" Adam said. "God! Freak out a little more, why don't you? What's the big deal?"

Jenna glanced at Stephanie and Marissa, who were laughing and whispering. The big deal was that Marissa was supposed to be hanging out with *her*. But once again, one of her siblings had to come along and ruin her afternoon for her.

"Just forget it," Jenna told Adam.

"Well, if you want help with your diving, I can help you," Adam offered.

Like I really want my twin brother coaching me. How humiliating, Jenna thought.

"Thanks, anyway," she said.

"Come on, Jen, I'm already at blue level," Adam said. "I can help."

"Oh, you're so cool," Jenna snapped back. "You're already at *blue* level."

I would kill to be at blue level, she added silently.

"I'm sorry I'm ahead of you, all right? But if you don't learn how to dive, you're going to be stuck back here in yellow while the rest of your friends move on to green and blue," Adam said.

Like I don't know this, Jenna thought, heat prickling at the back of her neck. Why couldn't everyone just leave her alone? Why did they have to keep reminding her of what a failure she was?

I want to call Mom, Jenna thought, then felt like a big baby. Her mother had plenty of other things to worry about this summer. She didn't need her daughter calling her up to whine about diving like she was some kindergartner.

"Come on. I'll practice with you," Adam said.

"Thanks, anyway, but I don't need your help," Jenna said, backing up. Thinking about her mother had made the hot prickling move into her eyes. "I'm fine."

"Jenna—"

"Really, Adam," Jenna said, turning. She had to get out of there before she started crying in front of everyone. "Just leave me alone!"

She turned and jogged to the beach, grabbing up her board shorts and flip-flops from the end of the pier. Jenna would have loved to have run back to the bunk and cried her eyes out, but she wasn't allowed to leave the lake area during free swim. The rest of the girls from 3C were lounging over by the first-aid shack and swimming in the shallow end, but she couldn't face her friends when she was all red-eyed and upset. Instead, she headed for a huge oak tree behind the water-sports cabin. She dropped to the ground in front of it, pulled her knees up under her chin and hugged them to her.

I am so sick of my brothers and sisters, Jenna thought, burying her face behind her legs. *Next year, I'm going to a different camp. Or better. I'll make Mom and Dad send all of them to a different camp.*

"Jenna? Are you okay?"

Sniffling quickly, Jenna looked up to find Chelsea hovering over her.

"I'm fine," Jenna said grouchily.

Chelsea tucked her blonde hair behind her ear and sat down next to Jenna. After two weeks at camp, Chelsea already had a deep tan, and the freckles across the bridge of her nose were more defined. She wore a baby blue bathing suit that brought out the stunning color of her eyes. In fact, Jenna now realized, all of Chelsea's bathing suits were blue, and for the first time she wondered if Chelsea had matched her eyes on purpose. Jenna looked down at her own bright suit. Matching her clothes to her eyes was something she never would have thought of doing. But that was Chelsea.

"Hey, I'm sorry I picked on you before," Chelsea said, putting her arm around Jenna. "I didn't know it was such a big deal."

"It's not," Jenna replied automatically.

"Okay," Chelsea said quickly.

They both stared at the ground for a moment.

Jenna watched a trail of ants returning to their anthill in a perfect line.

"I am so glad I don't have a brother," Chelsea said finally.

"Adam is such a jerk," Jenna replied. " 'I'm in blue, you know.' Like we don't *all* know he's ahead of the rest of us."

"He's so obnoxious," Chelsea agreed. "We need to get back at him."

Jenna lifted her head fully for the first time. Chelsea's eyes gleamed with mischief. "Get back at him? How?"

"Nothing big," Chelsea said with a shrug. "Just a small, innocent prank. To remind him who he's dealing with."

Jenna smiled slightly. A prank. Yes. That would make her feel better. Pulling a prank always made her feel better. It would take her mind off diving, off Adam and Stephanie, off her parents. She grinned at Chelsea. Just that morning, Jenna had been beyond mad at the girl, but suddenly that didn't matter anymore. If there was one thing Chelsea was good for, it was pranking. She was fearless and smart, the perfect partner-in-crime. And that was exactly what Jenna needed at the moment.

"We need a plan," Jenna said. "A really, *really* good one."

▲ ▲ ▲

Chelsea and Jenna stood in the bathroom that evening, huddled in the corner by the second toilet. It had started to drizzle outside toward the end of free swim, and the light rain tapped against the windowpane above their heads. As always, the rain brought out the slight moldy smell of the bathroom and made the air thick. Out in the bunk, the rest of Jenna's friends killed the free time before dinner by writing letters to their parents and friends. Jenna, however, was doing what she did best—plotting.

"Are you sure you can do this?" she asked Chelsea under her breath. "I can if you want me to. I can fake it better than anybody."

"I know, but Julie's never going to believe you have a stomachache," Chelsea said. "You're you."

"Yeah. I guess I have used it too many times," Jenna said, checking her plastic watch. "Okay, we gotta do it now, or we won't have time."

"Let's go," Chelsea said with a nod.

Jenna lifted a twenty-ounce bottle of Sunkist her dad had sent in a care package. She nodded at Chelsea, who coughed so that no one would hear the hiss as she popped the bottle open. Then Jenna nodded again, and Chelsea started making some of the most convincing barfing noises Jenna had ever heard.

Stifling a laugh, Jenna dumped the Sunkist into the toilet so it would sound like Chelsea was actually throwing up. When they heard an "Ew" and some movement in the bunk, Jenna tossed the bottle into the trash, and Chelsea hit her knees, quickly flushing the toilet. Seconds later Julie appeared in the doorway with half the bunk gathered behind her.

"Who's sick?" Julie asked, her eyes darting to Chelsea.

Chelsea took a deep, heaving breath. Her hair

stuck to her forehead as she looked up at Julie with heavy eyes.

"I don't feel so good," Chelsea said.

"She threw up. A lot," Jenna confirmed, doing her best grossed-out face.

Julie crouched next to Chelsea and pushed her hair back from her face. Jenna was impressed to see Chelsea swallowing hard and hanging her head. The girl knew what she was doing. If Jenna didn't know better, even *she* would have believed Chelsea was ill.

"Can you make it to the nurse's cabin?" Julie asked.

"I don't know," Chelsea said weakly.

"I'll take her," Jenna volunteered. As if the idea had just come to her.

Julie helped Chelsea to her feet, where she stood leaning sideways slightly like she was about to fall over.

"Chelsea? Do you need me to go with you, or is Jenna okay?" Julie asked.

"No. Jenna's fine," Chelsea said, adding a burp. "You have to take everyone to dinner." She put her hand over her stomach and grimaced. "Uh. Dinner."

"I better get her out of here before she ralphs again," Jenna said, wrapping her arm around Chelsea. Together, they staggered to the bathroom door, where everyone parted to let them through.

"Here, you guys," Grace said, helpfully grabbing their windbreakers from the pegs by the door. "It's raining out, and you don't want Chelsea to get even sicker."

"Thanks," Jenna said, feeling a little guilty over Grace's concern and thoughtfulness. She and Chelsea struggled into their jackets and headed out into the drizzle.

"Feel better!" Brynn called after them.

Then the screen door slammed shut, and Jenna and Chelsea made their way around the bunk. As soon as they were safely out of sight, Jenna stopped pretending to hold Chelsea up, and they took off at a run, heading for the mess hall. The plan was simple, but it had to be done within the next five minutes, or they were sure to get caught.

Jenna's heart pounded as her feet slammed along the muddy path through the woods. She loved this energized feeling she got whenever she was about to pull a prank. She was half psyched, half nervous, but couldn't stop grinning. When Jenna was pulling a prank, it was like the rest of the world and all its problems melted away. All that was left was fun.

Chelsea emerged into the clearing behind the mess hall first. Jenna looked both ways. The coast was clear. They sprinted to the back of the building and leaned against the wooden planked wall.

"Whew. Made it," Chelsea said, wiping some rain off her cheek.

"I'll peek inside," Jenna offered.

As always, the back door to the kitchen was open to let the air in while the cooks slaved over the hot stoves. Ever so slowly, Jenna checked around the side of the door. The three cooks and Pete were all standing at the huge silver stoves, talking and laughing as they stirred huge vats of torture food.

Ugh. Smells like beef Stroganoff, Jenna thought, scrunching up her nose. This would be one of those bread-only nights for her, but it was good news for the prank. Her brother *loved* that gooey brown mess.

"Jenna! Come on!" Chelsea whispered.

Pulse pounding in her ears, Jenna reached up to the shelf next to the door and grabbed a five-pound bag of sugar. She was pressed back into the outside wall again before anyone was the wiser.

"It's so great how they keep all that stuff right by the door," Chelsea said.

"I know. It's like they're *asking* us to steal it," Jenna replied, hugging the bag to her.

"Okay, let's go," Chelsea said.

Crouching low below the windows, Jenna and Chelsea made their way around the side of the mess hall to the front. Mud splattered Jenna's sneakers, and rain dripped from her hood onto her nose. When they reached the door, Chelsea peeked inside and quickly jumped back.

"The CITs are still setting the tables," she informed Jenna.

"Count to ten and check again," Jenna said.

Together, they counted up to ten Mississippis, then Chelsea checked.

"Okay! They're all back in the kitchen. It's now or never," Chelsea said.

They locked eyes, filled with excitement. Then Jenna nodded. "Go!"

Jenna and Chelsea ran into the mess hall, right over to Adam's table. There were three sets of plastic salt and pepper shakers, and Jenna grabbed them all up while Chelsea slid under the table. Jenna joined her and opened the salt bottles while Chelsea ripped open the bag of sugar. They sat, cross-legged and facing each other. That was when Jenna noticed a snag in the plan.

"What do I do with the salt?" Jenna whispered, her heart pounding wildly.

"Oh, God! Why didn't we think of that?" Chelsea asked.

Jenna looked around and was hit with an idea. "My pockets!"

"Nice!" Chelsea replied.

Quickly, Jenna emptied all three salt shakers into her jacket pockets. Chelsea grabbed the bottles one by one and dipped them into the sugar bag to fill them.

"This is gonna be so great," Chelsea said with a snicker.

"I know!" Jenna whispered back.

Just as Jenna was replacing all the shaker tops, they heard the door from the kitchen bang open.

Jenna froze, a chill of fear sliding over her from head to toe. Chelsea grabbed her hand. Their palms were both covered in sweat—or maybe it was just rain. Either way, Jenna could practically hear her friend's heart beating.

"You were supposed to make sure all the glasses from lunch got cleaned!" someone scolded. "What are we supposed to do with ten dozen dirty glasses?"

"Whatever. It's too late now. Don't say anything and no one will notice," another voice answered.

Jenna and Chelsea both stuck out their tongues. So much for drinking any bug juice tonight. The two sets of feet clomped right by their table and out the front door.

"That was close," Chelsea said.

Jenna nodded. "Let's get out of here."

They checked first to make sure the coast was

clear, then quickly replaced all the salt and pepper shakers on Adam's table. It was all Jenna could do to keep from laughing out loud as they raced out the front door and turned their steps toward the nurse's cabin.

"Omigosh! This is going to be so funny!" Chelsea cried, dumping the rest of the sugar in the nearest garbage can.

Jenna shook the salt out of her pockets and it rained down, disappearing into the grass. "I know! Beef Stroganoff is bad enough, but beef Stroganoff with sugar? Gag me!"

"Come on! We have to get to the nurse's station and tell her I was sick, but the fresh air cured me," Chelsea said. "There's no way I'm missing this!"

They grabbed hands and ran for the nurse's station to cover their tracks in case Julie followed up with Nurse Helen later. Jenna could barely wait to get to dinner. So much for Adam thinking she couldn't pull a prank on him. He had no idea what was about to hit him!

Read more in

camp CONFIDENTIAL

Jenna's Dilemma

available now!